AF487155

Deena Kaye

Copyright 2024

Black Willow Publishing

WHISPERS

WHISPERS

CHAPTER 1

Pia

Her dark brown hair fell like a curtain over her left eye, stubborn as a petulant child with a will of its own. She brushed it away annoyingly, out of habit, the hair falling again, with defiance, right where it wanted. She flung the garbage bag, laden with wasted food and greasy remains from the grill, high into the air where it landed with a resounding wump in the dumpster, against a clatter of empty cans, old liquor bottles, and cardboard what nots the feral cats would soon enjoy rummaging through.

Pia brushed off the remnants from the leaky bag that stuck to her apron. She liked her physique. The roughhewn timber of her at 5'11' gave her strength. She took pride in the strong bone features and flat chest, with long legs and mussed hair that she once again shook, using her fingers to momentarily clear her vision revealing large, soft brown eyes.

"FUCK! I locked myself out again!" She growled, stomping her way to the alley to find the hidden key to front door of Kramer's Grill and Chill café.

Three months of working here at this highway grease spot was getting no easier. She was forever grateful Mr. Kramer took her in, no questions asked, but she was always on high alert. She couldn't leave the state, had nowhere to live, and had to keep a job. The concern was, what if someone recognized her?

Pia entered the faintly lit café, with its polished Formica counter gleaming from the forceful glimmer of the outside utility pole light. She snapped an aluminum window shade closed against any curious travelers that might have any doubt that the lack of neon glare, and closed sign, really meant closed. *No one here, go away.* Tonight was not a night she wanted to indulge some wayward, weary tourist as they pleaded for a bowl of soup or a sandwich to continue on their way. She felt a twinge of bitterness for they had a destination that heralded freedom of

some sorts for them, taken for granted by
them and surely unappreciated by them
she was sure. And as ever, she gave into
their needs, for why should everyone
suffer?

Continuing her path to the kitchen,
she turned off the remaining light,
symbolizing her departure. She felt
contrite. As her back throbbed with pain,
she yearned for the comfort of a
refreshing shower and the presence of
someone to chase away her loneliness. So
lonely, the ache of it caused a growth of
bitterness in the cavity of her chest.

But, the bitterness that grew in her
mind, was more for the lack of justice
and blindness of a southern culture too

supercilious to embrace the rest of the world and its norms. She shut out the pain with a bite to her lower lip.

"Oh, for crying out loud!" Pia noted with frustration. A second smaller black bag of garbage sat next to the door. She would need to make a second trip to the dumpster. As she exited the building, she firmly closed the metal door with a clang, checking for its locked nature, intentionally this time. She patted her chest pocket with relief, noting the firm, rugged shape of the spare key. A distracting blur of motion caught her eye, and she glanced with a sense of fear toward the dumpster.

Silence.

Five trotted steps and a large swing of her arm brought the small bag up and over into the receptacle.

"OUCH!"

Pia halted in shock. Her mouth hung open, and she froze. Her eyes widened in even more surprise when a small, dark headed young woman peered over the rusted, metal rim.

Pia couldn't help but find it a bit humorous to see the disgruntled girl's mishap with hair askew and banana cream pie smeared across her mouth. Such an unexpected pleasure, and a travesty all at the same time. Her shoulder length, black as coal, hair fell into her face and stuck on a whipped cream disaster laden on her cheek. The girl's futile attempt to quickly wipe away the mess only resulted in further smearing, as the goo found its way onto her wire-rimmed glasses, delicately balanced on her nose.

Pia took a tentative step toward the apparent fugitive. "Hey ...-."

With lightning speed, the young woman hefted herself over the edge of the metal encased takeout diner and bolted toward the darkened alley leading to the front parking lot.

"What a second! I just wanna..."

There was a sickening thud, crunch, and then silence, before the girl toppled backwards from smacking into the corner of the brick wall. The banana cream pie had blocked just enough of her vision to be the root of the ensuing fiasco.

"Oh, no." Concern replaced amusement as Pia ran to help the girl up. "Here. It's okay! Come on. Give me your hand."

"My glasses!"

"Yah, they took quite a hit. Not to mention your forehead. That's going to be a goose egg." Her eyes confirmed what the girl could not see. A spot on her forehead was swelling with an egg-shaped bulge.

The girl moved away, but her effort wasn't very convincing. Pia's voice softened. "Let's go inside where you can get cleaned up and I can make you something decent to eat."

The girl attempted to push her glasses up along her nose as she looked toward the area that would lead to the front door, calculating her decision, when the bridge of her glasses cracked, rendering them useless. She sighed with despair.

Pia stood with confidence and authority. Holding out her hand in a firm gesture of support, she added,

"Come on, I'll help you up." She pulled the sullen girl to her feet. "No one is around this time of night. You'll be safe with me."

She released the stranger's hand she noted she was still holding and strode to the alley, allowing the woman to follow. Pulling out the spare key from her pocket, Pia said to herself, thank God I had a second bag of garbage, who knows what would have happened to this vagabond.

Pia guided the young lady to the bathroom to freshen up while she attempted to tape her glasses back together in some misshapen form that would suffice for a visual aid. She was staring at the kitty wampus excuse of a frame when the girl re-entered the dining area.

"Are you sure no one else is coming around?"

"Not till four. Plenty of time!" Although Pia was not sure what plenty of time would be needed for. "What's your name?"

"Jae-sang." She replied with automation, then looked regretfully at her disclosure. Her head turned in an attempt to deflect unwanted questions.

Pia spoke the name aloud, testing her pronunciation. "Tsay-sung."

"Not bad, but just call me Jay, it's easier." She sat on a stool at the counter, looking casually around. "Can I get something to drink?"

"Sure!" Pia said exuberantly. "What would you like? Water? Tea?" She waved her arms toward the back grill. "I've got rice. Would you like me to cook you some rice?" She enticed.

"Are you fucking serious right now? Please tell me you're joking. No! Don't tell me that. Let me just assume you're an ignorant asshole, like every other round eye around here!"

Pia stood stunned. What had she said? She was at a loss as to why Jae was so riled. "I just thought you might like rice because you're ... well, you know…"

"Korean?" Jae's face flushed, and her lips pressed tight.

Pia's continued dumbfounded expression conveyed it all.

"I'm an American, you idiot! I was born here."

"Sorry," Pia said, contrition laced her voice.

"So ignorant." Jae turned her attention to a newspaper on the counter. She growled.

"I guess." She hesitated with embarrassment. "So, do you want-."

"A hamburger." She continued to peruse the paper. "No! Make it a CHEESE burger!" She said with exuberance. She glanced at Pia with forgiveness written across her face.

"Okay," stated with relief. "Fries?"

She looked up again, this time beaming, a lustful leer to her grin. "YES! And onion rings and ooh, can I have a strawberry milkshake?"

"Sure. I'll get right on that. Uh, the newspaper, can you...?"

"Oh, yah! Koreans can read."

Pia sighed with frustration. "No. I meant because of your glasses."

"Oh, right." Jae's voice was soft with apology. "My turn. Sorry."

Pia handed her the flimsily taped frame of glass and wire. Jae, graciously accepted. A small smile of appreciation accompanied her relaxed face. Pia turned to the grill to get the feast underway.

Chapter 2

Pia and Jae

Pia had never seen anyone so tiny
pack in so much food. She just didn't
stop. Although petite in nature, and a
fine display of manners, Jae ate nonstop
for 22 minutes, finishing every morsel on
her plate and, with politeness, slurped
the last of her milkshake accompanied by
a modest belch contained behind her
diminutive but well-manicured fingers.

Out of politeness, Pia ate a bowl of
beef and barley soup hoping it would
make her feel less conspicuous. She
needn't have worried! Jae ate with relish
while reading and re-reading the local

newspaper with no inkling of concern. Pia noted the expensive, layered haircut that fell just to her shoulders. Jae wore high-quality designer clothing, clearly not local. Her back pack was a Guess brand indicating a city girl from at least 200 miles away.

"Who are you hiding from?"

"No one."

"You just like dumpster diving for day old pie, is that it?"

"Maybe."

Pia wiped the Formica and pulled dirty dishes from the counter before she continued. "How's your head?"

Jae's finger tips gently tapped at the swelling. "Sore." Again, her eyes remained on the newspaper, not encouraging more conversation, but not conveying rudeness either.

"Look, I gotta close up here. We open again in a few hours." She looked expectantly at Jae. "I can give you a lift somewhere."

With that, she folded up the paper and looked directly at Pia. "That would be great."

The moon, with its halo of glistening moisture, embraced its crescent shape of milky white, signaling the end of its nightly shift as it hung low in the velvety sky. The 1999 Ford Explorer, despite its wear and tear with 278,000 miles on its odometer, started up effortlessly.

Pia didn't ask where to go, she just drove along the highway, their merger an unspoken partnership of comfortable quiet.

After a while, Jae broke the silence, her voice tinged with a hint of desperation. "I don't have a place to go. Can I stay at your place? Just for the night, please!" Her voice rose with intensity. "I promise I won't be a bother, and I'll be gone by lunchtime at the latest."

Pia's response was silence, her eyes fixed on the road. Eventually, she veered off the highway towards the Super 8 motel. "I can get you a room here, if you'd like," Pia offered.

Jae looked with uncertainty at the darkened structure. "Where do you live?" Her question was innocent enough.

Pia continued to gaze out of the windshield, a lengthy pause hanging in the air. "I can't have you stay with me. It's not the best of accommodations," she finally replied.

"I don't mind. I'll sleep on the floor! I can cook, clean. Whatever!" Jae pleaded, urgency in her voice. Fear was evident in her eyes.

The engine idled, and they sat together in the motel parking lot, observing the hookers coming and going from dilapidated rooms. Even at this late hour, the sounds of Johns pulling their vehicles into vacant spots for clandestine moments of costly pleasure filled the air.

Jae broke the silence once more, her voice heavy with the weight of her past. "Not long ago, I came here in search of maid work. They tried to hook me up with a job as a 'hostess,' when the maid position didn't work out." Jae shook her head in disgust. "I just couldn't do it. The thought of putting some guys' dick in my mouth just made me want to vomit."

Pia looked at her with empathy.

"I live in my car."

"You do?" Jae sounded incredulous. When Pia's face revealed her emotions, Jae stated with forced support. "Oh! No judgement." But, in a softer voice, Jae added with honesty, "well kinda surprised." She looked sheepish.

A small lump of shame choked in Pia's throat as the adverse memory of her five by six foot cell poured into her mind. The fear and helplessness of waking up in a hospital after being knocked on the head that night many years ago was something she often buried in her subconscious. When she gained her composure, Pia shrugged her shoulders trying to appear gallant. She looked toward the back of her spacious Explorer. "I've got plenty of room, if you don't mind sharing the space."

"Heck no! Beats the ground any day."

It only took a minute for Pia to set up the sleeping bags and lay out extra blankets. With the back seats folded down, there was plenty of space for them to sleep in. Pia glanced out the side window and saw Jae going through an elaborate nighttime routine of brushing her hair, wiping her face, cleaning her teeth, and changing her underwear. Jae hopped into the car with a burst of energy. "Aren't you going to freshen up?" she asked.

"Already did, back at the café," Pia lied, knowing that Jae was probably aware.

"Oh, well, I'm ready whenever you are," Jae replied. Without waiting for an answer, Jae hurried to the back and slipped under the covers. She asked Pia, "Are you sure you don't mind sleeping next to another girl? I can sleep up front."

Pia stifled a laugh. "No, not at all. I have two other sisters and I've always shared a room with at least one of them." Pia methodically took off her outer shirt, revealing a tank top underneath. She then removed her jeans and hung them on the hook above the passenger window. Just as Pia was about to get into her sleeping bag, Jae spotted a small crimson light piercing through the darkness. "What's that light thing?"

Sighing with frustration, she answered, "It's a leg monitor. On parole. Got early release if I wear this thing for 6 months, and keep a job."

"Oh."

Pia tries to read her thoughts without success.

"Parole huh? Not an axe murderer or anything like that, are you?"

"Too late for you, if I am."

She laughs, but looks nervous.

"Come on, I'm beat. Gotta get some sleep. Cops come around early sometimes. I'll have to move the car if they do." Pia snuggled in, sure to fall asleep readily. She felt utterly exhausted.

Just as she felt the curtain of slumbered bliss cover her inner eyes, the sound of a guttural growl brought her attention full tilt awake. The growl came again, followed by a softer percussion sound, like a puff.

Pia raised her head and looked out the tinted windows in concern, when the sound echoed again, emanating beside her, where Jae lay in deep slumber, snoring.

CHAPTER 3

The Butlers

The sound echoed ominously through the open window, a haunting familiarity that sent a twist in his gut. He couldn't ignore it, drawn toward it like a moth to a flame, needing to uncover its source.

Ryan glanced furtively through the window as he passed. She sat there, her arms crossed as a way to stifle the pain. She wasn't crying. No tears escaped her eyes this time, for she knew there was no escape from his relentless assault. The shock and fear that had once gripped her had now transformed into self-pity and anguish, her desperation growing with each event. Her cousin, caring little for the pain he inflicted upon her, was now somewhere filing a jug with more homemade hooch. Liquid courage, giving permission to hit a woman and more than once if even to relieve his boredom. The more she argued, the more he hurt her, a vicious cycle, an endless loop of torment. Ryan glanced away, noticing even the curtain fought desperately to escape, only to be pulled back by the feeble breeze. It hung limp, a symbol of its own resignation, just as Kelly must feel. The whole ass backward country bumpkin world around here seemed to know of the atrocities committed by that despicable man, yet no one dared to intervene. It was a sickening display of the twisted traditions that ran in this family's blood.

Ryan's imagination using black plastic bags and duct tape with Waylen wrapped up in it flooded his mind. But he knew his duty as an observer, bound by his job description, prevented him from sinking to the level of these Neanderthals. He had to be patient, biding his time, waiting for justice to prevail.

"Hey, Ryan!" A sharp whistle followed, as Stan, the leader of the Neanderthals, stood in the shadows of the late-night outdoor Hillbilly campsite, impatiently waving at him. Whistles and waves seemed to be their preferred form of communication.

As Ryan approached, he expected a grunt from Stan, but to his surprise, Stan actually spoke a complete sentence. "Time for a meetin.' Where's Waylen?"

Ryan pointed toward the one-room cabin, and Stan followed his gaze.

Wait for it...

Pushing air from his vocal cords, Stan emitted a grunt without opening his mouth.

There it is.

Two short whistles came forth, each unique to signal the recipient. And this one called for Waylen.

With heavy steps, Stan made his way to the fire pit, where a low blaze lay waiting like the furls of hell to be stoked or diminished. Stan threw two logs on. Furled it is. This was going to be a long meeting.

The homemade whiskey passed around the circle again. Ryan pretended to take a long swig of the rock gut, adding an exaggerated, 'Ahhh,' as he passed the saliva soaked Mason jar on to the next family member.

"You boys gotta keep your eyes open, listen to what's being said, or not said." He belched.

Ryan was pretty sure you heard with your ears, not your eyes, but maybe the Butlers had a secret power he didn't know about. After living amongst them for the last three years, he was pretty sure their IQ of 70 tops nullified that idea.

Stan continued with angry words and spittle that flew like punctuations into the embers. "Someone's busting our balls. There's a leak."

Ryan and Waylen looked incredulously at the magisterial idiot. An idiot that was dangerous.

"We got our stash seized up at Moon Shine Beach. Somebody tipped the cops."

Ryan said with edged regret. "We spent so much time on that deal. Rat bastards!"

"Exactly!" Stan approved of Ryan's explanation with a finger point and head nod as the jar came to his lips again for a deep swig.

Oh dear God, how did this family make the money they made and continue to live for generations as they did without ever getting one iota smarter?

"The preacher ain't gonna like it, that's for damn sure!"

Waylen added his importance, "Maybe, it's someone from his group."

"Nah. He didn't know about this extra run we was makin'." He pulled his bloodshot eyes up to meet Ryan's. "But, I believe I know just who- it- is."

Ryan's throat went dry. He remained passive on the outside, but was already thinking three ways to run. A small smoldering stick laying in the fire which could easily be used as a club for one of the two caught his eye. His thoughts were interrupted.

"Didn't you send that kid up to Silver Dollar City?"

"Yah." Ryan waited for the connection of the statements, but none were forthcoming.

"Waylen!"

His head snapped up. His eyes tried to focus on his older brother.

"You're making the next run to Branson. But tell the kid we're sending cash down to Table Rock. Ryan, you'll go up to Branson and see what shakes loose."

"Gotcha! Good plan."

Belch. "Damn right!" He stood a bit unsteady, and turned toward his cabin. "Dismissed."

Waylen toppled over backward in a stupor, remaining prone. Ryan walked slowly, with pretense of drunkenness as well, toward his bunk in the larger cabin he shared with Waylen, but not tonight.

He knew the well-trod path by heart and stood strong and tall as he turned the corner, edging away from the fire's light. His covert flight was interrupted by the presence of Kelly carrying a bucket of water from the creek on her way back to her cabin. He jerked to a stop, ready to step into the foliage, but she already saw him.

With a half-smile, she looked expectantly at him. "Hey, Ryan."

His eyes turned from the welted face and bruising eye to the half torn dress, still laying off her shoulder.

"Oh," she stuttered, as she pulled the sleeve back up. "I could sure use a hand," she added, trying to sound casual. Still, her eyes revealed a desperate plea for recognition. Someone to rescue her.

Ryan hesitated. He didn't dare look too eager to move on. He also could not reveal his awareness of her cousin's temper. With misgiving, he replied, "Sure thing, Kelly. I was wondering where you were at." He kept his voice light and pleasing. "You missed the meeting."

Her voice was strained, and she avoided his eye. "I already knew what Stan was worrying over. I had to fix up biscuits for tomorrow."

They walked back in silence he carrying the bucket; she trying to keep close, hoping he would change hands on the handle so she could grab his hand and hold it.

He knew better, his stride long and quick. As they reached her brightly lit house in the woods, she spoke warmer, with falseness. "Got some dumplings heatin' up, Ryan. You're welcome to come in and fix a plate. I know you boys didn't eat none."

"Gosh Kelly, sounds real good." He jostled his stature in anxiety. "I got stomach problems. I gotta head to the outhouse. Maybe tomorrow'." He nodded to her for acceptance.

Her face twisted up in displeasure at the thought of his absence and the reason for it. "Well, good night then." She turned back with hope, "See you tomorrow?"

"You know it!" Turning quickly, he strode away into the night before she could make him promise more.

CHAPTER 4

Jack and Ryan

The patrol car eased in through the heavy brush. Far enough off the dirt road to camouflage the reflective lettering, close enough for a quick getaway if needed. He sat in the stillness for several minutes, eyes straining through the brush for any movement. He had just enough time before his shift ended and daybreak exposed his cover. Time seemed to stretch as he waited, his heart pounding in his chest, fueled by a mixture of excitement and apprehension.

With stealth, he slipped out of the vehicle, his movements as light as a whisper. With each careful step, he made his way toward the ancient cottonwood snag, its silhouette barely discernible in the fading moonlight. Jack crouched down in the underbrush, hidden from view, and patiently waited.

The air was heavy with anticipation as he finally heard the faint, cautious footsteps drawing nearer. He held his breath, feeling his heart thumping in his chest. Finally, a striking figure emerged from the dense foliage - a man with a wiry frame, his chestnut brown hair glinting under the moon's gentle glow. He paused, just as Jack had, his senses attuned to the surroundings, listening intently.

Jack let out a small hoot owl call. The man smiled. Jack stood and whispered, "Hey!" He continued out of the underbrush gingerly as to avoid any unnecessary noise, in case the sound carried to disagreeable persons.

In three long strides, the man found his way to Jack's embrace, and they kissed deeply.

His breath coming in heaves, he said hoarsely, "Anybody see you coming here?"

"Why do you always ask me that? If that was true, I wouldn't be here." He pulled at Jack's pants, wrestling with his uniformed belt buckle. He stroked softly

along the hard edge of Jack's cock,
pressing through the fabric. Jack let out a
soft, deep moan.

"Ryan!" He kissed him passionately.
Softer numerous kisses trailed along his
jaw, just below his earlobe, then back to
his mouth. "I'm off tomorrow. Think
you can make it to Forsyth? We can fuck
all day if you want." His smile was wide
in anticipation.

"Can't. Stan wants us to time a run to
Branson and back, then bulldog that café
owner up in Hollister. He wants to use
the restaurant as a drop since the
Greyhound bus comes through there
now, but the ole man's putting up a
fight. Clever plan to pick up and drop off

the meth, if you think about it." He continued to pull off Jack's clothing. "I feel sorry for the old man, though. Stan's got 'em over a barrel about some preachers' daughter he slept with 20 years some ago. He's got him believing he's got pictures and is gonna turn him in."

Jack grabbed both of Ryan's hands so he could concentrate. "Why the hell would he care about that? It's been 20 years."

Ryan took advantage of the use of his freed hands and undid his own belt, kicking off his shoes and sliding his jeans off, revealing a long, slender member quivering for Jack's attention. "Because the preacher is the main meth distributor for Shepherd of the Hills near Silver Dollar city. That guy would skin a cat alive and throw it at your grandma. He's got no feelings, no common sense, and no fear. He'd kill ole Bill just for spite."

Jack had just a second for pause before Ryan pulled his steaming mouth to Jack's and sucked on his tongue. They walked backwards with bodies pressed together, pulsating with desire, until, by memory, they found the straw filled pit they had made. They tumbled in, bodies shivering with desire.

"I've only got a few minutes." He said breathlessly. "Waylen's in a foul mood again and will probably be looking for a drinking buddy before we head out."

Jack pulled his head back. "Do not say that vile man's name while I have you in my mouth, please!"

Ryan looked at Jack appreciatively as he entered his throbbing cock once more between Jack's willing lips.

Exhausted from their effort, their shuddering bodies lay next to each other, spent and satisfied.

"I hate to spoil the moment and all, but we've got a situation." Jack rolled on his side to face Ryan with his head propped in his hand. "Kelly won't get off my ass with the flirting and shaking her tail around me. No way can I fake sex with her. I can't blow my cover." Affectionately, he pulled a piece of straw out of Jack's hair. "Even Stan's been hinting it'd be nice to have another man in the family. God, it gives me the heebie-jeebies." Ryan shuddered in disgust.

"Get her good and drunk. When she wakes up next to you, tell her she's the best you ever had. She won't know the difference." He looked at Ryan apologetically, "An egg white wouldn't be a bad idea to make it look like..., well, you know."

"Gross." He sighed. An edge of fear in his voice escaped him, "I can't do that every time."

"I know." Ryan rose to dress. "I can't wait for this to be over. This undercover work with the family from a Deliverance movie is getting real ugly. I'm worried for you."

Ryan pulled back to look at Jack with curiosity. "What Deliverance movie?"

"Oh shoot, you don't know? I wanted to play Burt Reynolds with you."

"Who's Burt Reynolds?"

"Dear God, you are a babe in the woods. But I won't hold that against you. Probably better you don't know. Too close to home. Speaking of which, when this is over…have you thought about us?"

"I think about us all the time."

"I mean coming out. Living together, in Forsythe."

Ryan's hesitation told Jack all he needed to know.

"This is going to end up like Brokeback Mountain."

"That was a fucked up ending."

Jack leaned down and kissed Ryan softly. "I don't want a fucked up ending for us." He finished tucking in his uniform shirt. "Think about it." He raised his arm with a half wave as he walked toward his squad car. "See you in a few days," he whispered.

CHAPTER 5

And The Truth Shall Set You Free

"What do you want to do with your life?" Jae asked while doing the crossword in the Sunday paper, in pen, mind you, while eating a mountain of pancakes, topped with blueberry pie mix. Jae had not asked about her parole as it seemed a sore subject and as long as Pia wasn't a serial killer or a baby snatcher, she could probably live with it, she surmised.

Pia swirled her spoon for the umpteenth time in her coffee. "Move as far away from here as possible and these small minded people." Pia's gaze wandered out to the endless flat fields of Hollister, Missouri population 35.

Thirty- six if you counted Jae. "What about you?"

"Same. But I'd like to hone my skills with technology. I used to do some hacking, surveillance stuff. You know, not the legit stuff, but now, I think a career in IT would really suit me." She met Pia's approving nod with her own.

"Just on your own?" Pia asked.

She shrugged her shoulders, letting her only recently inert fork dig deeper into the diminishing pancake stack.

Pia wanted to ask about her family, find out what made her run away, who she was, what kind of life she had, but she didn't want to spook her.

Ten days had passed since she had first met Jae. She found her to be intelligent, easygoing and never stopped talking, but Pia really enjoyed her company. Jae was keen to earn her way, so she waited tables while Pia cooked and it worked out pretty good. Mr. Kramer couldn't afford to pay her, so was agreeable to have her on, as long as she worked for tips and food.

Pia couldn't understand why a café as bustling as this one always seemed to be short on funds. The place was becoming dilapidated and desperately required several repairs. Although the restaurant

had been paid off a few years ago, Bill
somehow managed to scrape by with just
enough money. Pia felt unsettled when
she went to collect her paycheck a few
days ago and noticed that Mr. Kramer
had a black eye. He noticed her
inquisitive gaze and simply shrugged his
shoulders. He didn't pry into her affairs,
and she didn't pry into his.

*   *   *

"I really respect you, Jae." Pia spoke to
her through the order window while she
scraped the grill late one night. Jae was
counting out her tips, which she
voluntarily gave 20% of to Pia, and an
extra 10 bucks for gas. She was eating a
mix mash of food tonight; mashed

potatoes, chocolate cake, and steamed broccoli, in addition to a grilled tuna sandwich.

Pia, in awe, watched her eat it while she talked. "You work so hard and you never complain. I bet you were the oldest in your family."

"No, actually 2nd oldest. I have a younger brother and an older brother."

Pia smiled to herself. She had found the first crack. "It's hard to be successful to everyone else's standards," Pia baited.

"No, shit. My dad is a tyrant. So old school." She looked at Pia to see if she was listening.

Pia nodded to her in encouragement.

"I know I told you we're American, but my dad has some ideas about women that are from the dark ages. My mom never worked. Probably didn't want to. But I do! I wanted to go to college." She hesitated.

"I've always wanted to own a business." Pia let the silence play out.

After some time, Jae came to the kitchen to fix hot tea. "My dad has me set up to meet someone from his home town in Korea. An arranged marriage."

"I didn't realize people were still doing that."

"Oh yah. There's a lot of money in it and family expectation, especially if you're..."

She stopped there and Pia could see a mark of fear written on her face.

"I love my family too, but you can't change the old ways. You gotta hope someday they'll accept the *you*, that you are, just the way you are."

"But if my father catches me, before I turn 18, he'll send me to Korea and I'll be married off to some troll and unable to return to the states."

"That's horrible! I'd hide out too, if I were you," she said supportively. With apparent frustration in her voice Pia continued, "I know it's not your mom's fault, but I get so mad when moms don't empower their daughters to become more in life, believe that they can do and be more. Women have to stop the cycle of dad's demeaning daughters and allowing society to treat them like, well, like they're objects." She looked at Jae to see if she had said too much.

Jae simply nodded while continuing to organize her cleaning supplies at this point.

"What does your name mean?"

"You've said it many times."

Pia contemplated on what they have talked about the last few weeks. She was just about to speak when Jae interrupted her thoughts.

"If you say rice or Korea, I will kill you."

Pia laughed. "I wasn't even thinking that!"

"Respect."

"I do, respect you."

"My name. It means success, and respect. What does your name mean?"

"I have no idea."

The questions came easy now. Jae got out the mop bucket, hoping no more customers would come in for the last 45 minutes of business. "How old are you?"

"23." Pia said.

"For reals?"

"For reals."

"When is your birthday, Jae?"

"October 11th, two months from now."

"Cut me a piece of pie would you? I'll sit with you a bit." With only a short time left before they closed, Pia was hoping for an early exit. "We can keep you hidden for two more months, no sweat."

"Then, I want to move to Wisconsin." She leaned back in a booth, satisfied, sipping with her now cooled tea.

"Wisconsin?" Pia said, with bewilderment.

"The two of us? Best friends, hanging out in our own apartment. We could do that right?"

Pia felt a steel door of protection cover her heart. There were aspects of her life that Jae had yet to uncover, complexities that she feared she wouldn't comprehend or accept. Pia didn't want to face that kind of rejection.

With relief, her thoughts were momentarily interrupted as her attention was brought to the opening of the door with a jangle of the bell scrapping against the metal trim of the glass entryway announcing a new customer. Through the glass entryway, she caught sight of a slender young man wearing wide leg, hip hop jeans, and an oversized Nirvana t-shirt enter through the door.

What stopped her cold was his spikey, fluorescent tipped hair against a dark scalp, cut crew style. He had the bluest eyes. Too blue.

Pia felt a chill go down her spine.

Chapter 6

Willow

The purple and green neon light in the shape of a five fingered palm blinked with insistence, beckoning the insecure traveler to step in to where only Madame Laveau could offer solace to your insecure wonderings.

The hour was late. Way too late to be studying your destiny if fate had landed you in dire predicaments you were unsure how to get out of. Nervously, the platinum-haired young man sat in his car, his gaze fixated on the palm-shaped sign displaying the word "Psychic" underneath. The darkened glass adorned with layers of colored beads and old-fashioned chintz cotton curtains hid the dimmed light within.

Willow reached into the duffle bag beside him and pulled out a crisp $100 bill, knowing it was the fee she would demand. He had taken a bit of cash before this run, and no one seemed the wiser. Tonight would be no exception. Considering his upcoming needs, he decided to withdraw a bit more money to cover both a meal at the diner and the gas he would need later on. It would be a long trip to Table Rock. The pilfering would be worth it if Madame Laveau could rid him of these God awful dreams; tell him what they meant.

Willow stuffed the duffle bag behind the seat of the Geo Metro, then thought better of it and brought it along for safe keeping. His watch showed 7:15 PM. He made good time driving at top speed from Moon Shine Beach. The drop off wasn't until midnight. Plenty of time.

The scent of incense enveloped his senses as he stepped inside. Bright, semi-sheer draped scarves adorned numerous lamps, casting a hazy glow that mingled with the fragrant mist, cultivating an atmosphere steeped in enigma.

"Greetings, young man."

Willow's eyes squinted as he looked through the dense murk, his vision obscured by shadows. With cautious steps, he ventured further into the room, his heart pounding in his chest. The beaded strands hanging in the far doorway jingled and crackled, parting to reveal a stout Cajun woman, her gray hair piled high in a beehive, exuding an air of confidence. The scent of spices hung in the air, adding an exotic touch to the atmosphere. As Willow's gaze met the woman's stern expression, a sense of foreboding washed over him, causing his throat to tighten with unease. Her murmured words carried a suggestive undertone, further fueling his apprehension.

"You have worries on your mind. I can help you." She nodded, trying to gain his compliance.

Well, no shit. He thought to himself. Why else would anyone be here to have their palm read? He clenched and unclenched the money in his hand, letting second thoughts race through his mind. Just as he realized he was wasting his time, she spoke again.

"Dreams. Dat's why you here. Doze bad dreams o' yours."

His eyes popped wide in surprise.

"They make you sweat at night." She cackled and wiped her nose on the back of her hand.

Willow swallowed hard. She was for real. How else would she know that? The weight of the moment hung in the air, and he couldn't deny the reality of it. His arm rose involuntarily, the movement almost hesitant, as he slowly opened his hand, revealing the wadded gratuity. Madame motioned for him to join her, the creaking of the rickety wooden chair adding to the ambiance. The small, round table lent softness with a royal blue velvet cloth, its richness adding elegance to the otherwise modest setting.

She made a clucking sound with her tongue against the roof of her mouth. "Won't do no good to read yo' palm. You done played wit' da devil."

Feeling numb, he plunked in the chair. He couldn't take his eyes off of her. A tremor ran through him. Her mouth smiled, almost gleeful, but her eyes held tight in a stink eye. He wanted to leave, forget he ever came here and drive to finish the drop, get high and sleep until noon tomorrow. But he had to know. Where the dreams a premonition or just the effects of his daily diet of pot and Mountain Dew? His body held transfixed.

Madame's breath escaped her lips in a deep, snake-like hiss, as she prepared herself for the impending trancelike state. Her moans, elongated and low, reverberated through the room, resonating with an otherworldly intensity. With closed eyes, one moment and rolling to the back of her head the next, she mumbled incoherently, her words lost in the ethereal atmosphere.

Willow, overwhelmed by the intensity of the moment, felt his body drenched in a sudden wave of sweat, his trembling hands betraying his unease. Slowly, he rose from his chair, desperate for a quick escape, but before he could make his move, the psychic's hands slammed

down on the table with a resounding
thud.

Her eyes, now bulging with an eerie
intensity, seemed to pierce through the
veil of reality as she spoke in a voice that
sent shivers down Willow's spine, "I see a
black head with three eyes."

Willow grimaced, his face contorting
in displeasure. "What?"

Noting the unusual piercing blue of
his eyes, she swiftly and eagerly pulled
the crystal ball, adorned with delicate
etchings, sitting in the center of the
antique wooden table, towards her with a
quick snap of her hands. With great
intensity, she leaned in, her breath held

in anticipation, and peered into the globe, her eyes darting from right to left, searching for any sign, any trace. But within the mystical depths, Willow saw nothing. No shape or form revealed itself that would proffer an answer to his burning question. Suddenly, as if struck by a jolt of electricity, he startled, leaping a full mile in surprise, when she sat up straight, her spine rigid, and hissed loudly, her voice a chilling whisper that echoed in the dimly lit room.

"You shouldna' done it, but you did. Days no goin' back now." Madame Laveau continued to stare off into the distance, staring above his head. Curious, Willow glanced over his shoulder to see what had captured her gaze.

Her voice came low and slow. "Innocent soul. Innocent soul. Your careless ways, a price to pay. Innocent soul you took that night. Thoughtless greed, your life the toll."

He sighed. So dramatic. "Can we get back to the dreams? See, I-."

She cut him off. "That be demons, laughing at you. No rest for the wicked. No way to get out, less you drive." She stared at him now, her gaze intense, pleading at him. "Drive away, now. Don' stop till you see water. Your eyes will be the death of you." In a normal voice, she commanded, "That will be a hundred dollars." And held out her hand for payment.

He sprang to his feet. He felt confused, tricked. What a bunch of garbage, he flustered to himself. He tossed the money on the table. Grabbing the duffle bag, Willow yanked up his low rise, wide leg jeans with frustration. Regret washed over him, as he questioned why he had bothered to stop here at all. As he stormed towards the door, his anger intensified. The clang of the bell above it startling him, a jarring sound he hadn't noticed upon entering.

Outside, the air was heavy with the odor of exhaust fumes from truckers passing by and the scent of distant rain. He stomped toward his car, his steps heavy with frustration, his breath coming out in frustrated puffs. The car door opened with a grating sound, matching his mood, and he sank into the worn leather seat with a huff. As he settled in, his hand instinctively reached for the hidden compartment where he had left his gun. His fingers trembled slightly as he confirmed it was still there, relief washing over him. But as he glanced at his watch, his shock was palpable. The digital numbers read 9:15, and he realized he had been inside for exactly two hours. How had that happened? What had happened?

Driving like a madman, his tires screeched on the asphalt as he desperately tried to make up for lost time. The county road stretched out before him, its dark silhouette blending with the night sky. Frustration boiled inside him as he wound his way along the county road, cussing and swearing his bad luck at stopping, which now made him impossibly late for the drop. Each passing mile intensified his anxiety, causing his hands to shake uncontrollably on the steering wheel. The trembling spread throughout his entire body, a physical manifestation of his mounting stress.

Finally, the glowing lights of Kramer's Grill and Chill came into view. With a sigh of relief, Willow maneuvered his vehicle to the side, his breath shuddering audibly. The open sign still lit bright. The scent of comforting food wafted through the air into his open car window, enticing his senses and reminding him to take care. He needed sustenance.

Chapter 7

Pie, Pie, Me Oh My

Willow's lips curled into a small, mischievous smile as he glanced at the tall, brown-haired waitress. The fluorescent lights overhead cast a soft glow on his peculiar hair, causing her to react with a hint of surprise. It wasn't uncommon for people to feel uncomfortable around him because of the unusual glow of his hair, and he rather enjoyed it.

"Whatcha got for pie?" He said brightly as he swung a leg around a stool. Willow scooted forward on his round swivel seat, resting his elbows on the worn surface of the counter. His bloodshot eyes watered with anticipation. The sound of his voice filled the air, as there were no other patrons to muffle the sound.

"Well," Pia answered stiffly, as she pointed to her plate still on the counter with a half-eaten piece. "Pumpkin." She then pointed to a menu board above the back counter, "Coconut crème, lemon merengue, apple crisp, blueberry-."

A burst of excitement lit up his eyes as he asked, "You got blackberry? I like blackberry."

Pia nodded in confirmation.

He placed a crisp fifty-dollar bill on the counter. "With ice cream," he declared with gusto, his enthusiasm evident in his voice. "Make it warm!" He added, his tone softer and more earnest, "Please!"

Pia couldn't help but comment on the timing, "You just made it!" She retrieved the freshly heated pie from the microwave, a warm aroma of fruit filling the air. "We would have been closed in a few more minutes," she added, hoping her mention of closing would encourage him to eat, pay, and leave. Yet, he appeared oblivious to her subtle hints, his simpering smile exploring the diner's surroundings.

A sense of unease washed over Pia as something about him felt strangely familiar.

"I used to stop here a lot, before I worked nights," he offered, his voice carrying a nostalgic tone.

"Nights?"

"Yah! Got me a delivery gig now. Pays real good. Better than them hook ups in Branson. Don't have to stand on no street corner in the middle of a rain storm looking for dick."

Pia was amazed at his candor. He had no shame. She continued with curious empathy. "You didn't want a day job?"

He looked at her, pleased she wanted to know about him. "Nah. Too young. I'd get picked up by the po-po for sure. Not going back to that hell hole of a home or no juvie hall, that's for sure. Besides, tricking made for good money, too. But this here job, I can save me some money and head to Mexico. Live real fine. That's what they say." He dove into his pie with the melting ice cream.

Pia felt wooden. Her brain was on five-alarm status. "Branson, huh? You lived there?"

"Oh yah! My whole life, till I got myself caught up in a mess. Shoulda never been there." He stopped mid bite.

The words of the psychic choking in his throat.

"You okay?" She scrutinized him, fearful of what was coming next.

His eyes snapped to the present, his gaze heavy with sorrow as he bared his soul to her. "Took a quick pay to pull some cash out of a bowling alley. Fellas involved said the guy owed 'em for undelivered drugs. Branson's full of gang wannabe cartel." With urgency, he shoveled the pie in his mouth.

And there it was. Undeniable. Their stories converging, this night, in this diner. Two fated lives crashing together.

Pia, desperate to keep him talking said, "Here's some more ice cream. Can't have good pie without ice cream."

He looked at her with a questioned expression. "I am kinda in a hurry." He gulped what was in his mouth. "But, what the heck! I'm already late, what's a few more minutes? Pile it on."

Pia added two more scoops. With demur interest in her voice, she questioned, "You said you made a mess. What do you mean?"

"Well, see I was just 13. More or less on my own, but you know, cops looking for kids out past curfew. We was just 'sposed to be in, then out. But some chick came in. Guess she was the cleaner. Had a mop an all. Come in early." He licked his spoon and pushed his plate with some uneaten blackberry filling to the front of the counter. He sighed in contentment.

Pia could hardly contain herself. Those blue eyes. The luminescent hair that danced in the glow of dimmed lights. Her last night at the bowling alley. She thought the memory when she awoke in the hospital was from her concussion. Something she had dreamed. But those eyes! It was him! Could she possibly get her life back? Not the three years wasted in jail, but her self-respect, her freedom? "AND!" She snapped impatiently. "What happened?"

He looked disconcerted as he wiped his mouth on a napkin. "It was dark. She never saw it coming. Stan whacked her on the head and dumped one of the cash registers on her. Made it look like she fell while robbing the place. No one was the wiser. Poor sucker. I ain't never been in no bowling alley since." His face paled. *I see a black head with three eyes.* The words of the psychic. She had seen a bowling ball. The last of the pie crust stuck in his throat. How much did she really know? He would have to make another visit to her and force her to tell him.

Pia's body quivered with seething anger, her clenched fists trembling at her sides. Each breath she took came in short, ragged puffs, as if struggling to keep up with the intensity of her emotions. Sitting before her was a teenage kid, his presence igniting a glimmer of hope within her, but the weight of years spent behind bars and the shattered fragments of her former life couldn't be undone. The prospect of proving her innocence and finally being free from the suffocating grip of parole sent a surge of adrenaline through her veins.

"Whad you say your name was?" she asked in anticipation. Her heart thundered in her chest, the rhythm matching the fierce determination coursing through her.

Her hopes of finding out more about this young man were dashed when the door of the café opened and a tall, lanky, sandy-haired highway patrolman walked in. Pia's heart sank. Her palms grew clammy as she pondered the situation. How could she possibly get more information from him now?

Jack Faber noticed the kid with white tipped hair and the bluest eyes he had ever seen. He sits next to the kid and, after apologizing for the last minute stop, looks at the mostly eaten blackberry pie with melted ice cream and says to Pia, "I'll have what he's having."

Jae slid with furtiveness to the kitchen to avoid the watchful eye of the patrolman and plated the dessert. She whispered nervously through the order window at Pia, "it sure is a night for having pie."

Pia's mouth watered, but not for the pumpkin pie she had long since put in the dirty dish tub, but for the memory of the salty tang of the best pie she had not had for some time, cooch pie.

"If only." Pia said, half under her breath as she pulled the plate from Jae's delicate hands.

"What?" asked Jae.

"Nothing." She sighed as she turned around. Pia pulled the ice cream out for the last time that night while sullenly scooping out the ice cream.

No one noticed the worn-out, older model pickup truck creep through the parking lot, its once vibrant white color now faded and dull. As the vehicle inched forward, the café's radiant lights illuminated the bustling interior, offering a clear view of every person inside.

The man in the truck fixated on the young man, mesmerized by the familiar blue hue of his eyes. He watched as the boy ran his fingers through his lustrous platinum hair, meticulously adjusting the peak of his stylish haircut in the reflection of the tinted window. A duffle bag sat prominently on an empty stool, catching the attention of the vigilant patrolman. Meanwhile, the tall, brown-haired waitress effortlessly engaged the patrons in lively conversations, her movements accompanied by the rhythmic wiping of the counter never led her to glance at the parking lot. The atmosphere seemed relaxed, as if no one had a care in the world.

*   *   *

Pia lay underneath the blankets, the heat warming the room they decided to splurge on, but still she felt a tremor of chill run through her bones.

Jae crawled in beside Pia after her long, and careful bed time routine of freshening and cleansing. Pia appreciated how proud she was of herself and the self-care she did, even under the most arduous of circumstances.

Pia laughed a short laugh as Jae tussled the blankets on her side to get cozy. A second queen bed remained next to them, unused. Jae liked the security of Pia close, she had stated, and why waste the sheets and space just for one person? Pia smiled at that. Why indeed?

"That guy tonight. He got you rattled. Do you know him?"

Pia sighed. "Maybe. I think he might be connected to my case."

Jae was quiet in her thoughts. She rolled to look at Pia with interest, concern creased on her brow.

"Tell me."

For several seconds Pia remained stone faced. She had never shared her story with anyone. She felt she could trust Jae with her story, but not if it meant rejection. Still, with so much between them now, Pia felt there was a bit more courage on her part now to open up.

"I know it's so cliché to hear, but I really am innocent."

Jae stared intently at her.

Pia continued, "I used to live in Branson. Had a job cleaning businesses at night. Made pretty good money too." She pulled another pillow under her head to get comfortable. "I had a cancellation on one of my slow nights, so I hit the bowling alley early. Showed up at midnight instead of 2 a.m. Next thing I know I'm waking up in a hospital with my arm cuffed to the bed rail."

"That's awful! You must have had a crappy lawyer."

"Oh, they had this wrapped in the bag. I was arraigned, sent to the jail infirmary, and scheduled for sentencing within 10 days. Had a public defender that looked like he spent most of his nights and early mornings drinking out of a paper bag. He didn't give a shit."

"Where does that kid come into the picture?"

"I hadn't turned on the lights yet. There was a slew of neon glow in the pit area where I was setting up to vacuum when I got hit from behind. I turned around and as I was sliding to the ground before I passed out, I saw the strangest thing. A face, with neon like blue eyes. And the hair! It glowed." Her voice raised with intensity. "Now how many people do you think look like that? I thought it was part of my effects from the concussion. But now, tonight, here comes this kid telling a story like mine! He could prove my innocence."

"Wow! That would be incredible. Do you think he'll come in again?"

"Maybe. He said he's doing a new delivery route. Must come by the café now and then. I'll ask Mr. Kramer if he's seen him." Pia sighed in despair. "Even if he wanted to corroborate, that would put him at the scene, make him liable as well. Who would want to do that and face jail time themselves?"

"Speaking of jail ... tell me all the sordid details about sex with other women!" Jae said with a leer.

Pia chuckled. "That's quite an assumption." She changed the subject. "There's gotta be a way to get help with this. I wish that highway patrolman hadn't showed up." She focused inward, lost in her thoughts. "Maybe we could talk to..., what was his name...? Jack?"

"It's worth a shot. But not me. Too many questions would come my way. I don't exactly look like a Hollister tourist.

Maybe, you could talk to the police in Branson?"

She snorted. "Police! They were part of the rush to put me away. I was always getting harassed by them. Said they found a gun on me, so they wanted to pin me with an armed robbery." She rolled over to face Jae. With intensity burning across her face, she said, "I live in the south as a gay business woman, trying to make it on my own. No family, few friends, and a load of debt. The only thing that would have made and will make a difference to my defense is a boat load of money." Pia's stomach quivered with dread. How would Jae respond? Would she be put off? Disgusted? Afraid?

With tenderness, Jae brushed the bangs out of Pia's eyes and said in a whispered voice, "The cave you fear to enter holds the treasure that you seek." She rolled onto her back. "Trying again takes strength. I believe in you."

Pia rolled onto her back as well and pulled the covers to her chin. "Is that some kind of Asian wisdom from an ancient sage?"

"No. Joseph Campbell."

Pia sighed heavy in the dark, feeling very alone.

Jae reached over as she often did and found Pia's hand under the covers. As their eyes weighted with sleep, their

clasped fingers found solace in the night.

CHAPTER 8

I Heard a Whisper

The next morning, the young women found themselves lounging lazily in the hotel room, as the morning sun filtered through the heavy curtains, casting a warm glow in the room. The aroma of freshly brewed coffee wafted through the air, reminding them that breakfast was just around the corner. Jae decided to take another refreshing shower, while Pia made plans to visit the Food Mart to fetch coffee and Jae's favorite cake donuts, topped with a delicious sprinkle of cinnamon sugar.

As Pia entered her locked vehicle, she noticed a paper-thin, semi-transparent business card resting on her seat. Its front adorned with a majestic gold dragon bearing Korean lettering. Written in neat black ink, an ominous message caught her eye. It warned her to return the girl and promised a substantial reward, while mentioning dire consequences if she failed to comply.

Pia felt her body freeze in terror, her breath coming in short, rapid bursts. She frantically scanned her surroundings, searching for anyone who seemed out of place or suspicious. Panicking beginning to ensue, she drove to the nearby convenience store with haste, stealing glances at the hotel parking lot through the window. With a sense of urgency, she gathered coffee, snacks, and a newspaper, her palms growing sweaty as she fumbled to retrieve crumpled bills from her pocket. "Keep the change," she hurriedly muttered, as she dashed out of the store and leaped into her car, parking it swiftly upon reaching the hotel.

Back in the safety of the hotel room, Pia locked all the locks and added the chain to the door, ensuring maximum security. Nervously, she peered through the crack of the curtain, her eyes darting around, searching for any lurking strangers who might pose a threat.

The water in the shower continued to pour steam, filling the hotel room. Pia sat nervously on the edge of the bed, her heart pounding so loudly it echoed in her ears. She could feel the heat radiating from her flushed cheeks as she gripped the newspaper tightly in her trembling hands. With furrowed brows, she scanned the columns repeatedly, searching for any clue that might hint at the presence of something sinister.

The aroma of freshly brewed coffee filled the air, but as Pia took a sip, the scorching liquid burned her lips, causing her to wince in pain. She tried to steady her breathing, attempting to calm her frayed nerves and clear her racing thoughts. If they truly knew where she was, why hadn't they made a move yet? Why hadn't they confronted her or even Jae when they had the chance last night in the parking lot? Pia nibbled on a donut, not bothering to wait for Jae. Her mind was a chaotic maze of fear, worry, suspicion, and sheer panic. By the time Jae finally entered the room, wrapped in a towel, Pia had made a resolute decision not to disclose the unsettling contact she had received.

Jae settled down beside her on the bed, letting out a contented sigh. Handing Pia a brush, she grabbed her own coffee and donut, relishing in the simple pleasure of indulging in their morning ritual.

Pia began to delicately brush and braid Jae's hair, the rhythmic swishing sound of the brush soothing her. Sitting on the hotel bed, she couldn't help but take in the cheesy orange and yellow chenille bedspread, its soft texture under her fingertips providing a sense of comfort. The abstract cheap art on the wall, though not particularly attractive, added a touch of character to the room.

The exchange of a comfortable mattress, the hot shower, the scent of fresh soap, and the convenience of a nearby toilet made them feel like royalty in this momentary haven of the tacky hotel room. But above all, Pia cherished the scent of Jae, the subtle aroma of her soaped skin filling the air. Pia admired the radiant glow of Jae's skin after she vigorously dried herself, her gaze always drawn to the little mole at the base of Jae's neck, an insignificant detail that made Pia's loins ache.

With care, Pia tied a royal blue ribbon, secured with a kkoji, to complete Jae's look. She spoke with careful consideration, attempting to sound casual. "That highway patrolman didn't even spare a thought about who was in the kitchen last night." She glanced up at the mirror hanging on the wall, seeking to reassure Jae with her eyes. However, a shadow of doubt or hurt crossed Jae's face, leaving Pia uncertain of its origin. Her intended words of comfort failed to provide solace, the memory of the ominous business card with the 'dire consequences' still lingering in her mind. She felt guilty as though she were lying to Jae by not revealing it.

Jae also furtively observed Pia's reflection in the mirror, her eyes tracing every detail of her face. As she studied her, she longed to understand this woman who held the safety of her life in her hands. The memory of waking up that morning, their fingers still intertwined as they lay side by side in bed, filled Jae's heart with warmth.

"If we had enough money," Jae started, her voice tinged with hope, "we could hire a better attorney and-."

Pia interrupted, determination in her voice, "That's a done deal. But if we can convince Willow to admit he was there, maybe I can finally get off parole. It would be one less thing for people to whisper about."

With an empathetic frown, Jae looked at Pia, trying to reassure her. "It must be incredibly difficult," she said softly. "Just being yourself, in your own skin, while others judge and refuse to accept you."

Pia let out a snort of frustration. "It's the norm for the rest of the world," she replied bitterly. "I feel normal, but it's frustrating and lonely when your sense of normalcy clashes with everyone else's. I tend to be a loner. Play it safe."

Understanding Pia's struggle, Jae nodded in agreement. "I know exactly what you mean," she said empathetically.

Pia continued, not hearing Jae's pain, her own voice filled with passion. "Have you ever seen a gay person tell a straight person that they are wrong, that they should change their sexual orientation? No! It's the other way around, without fail. What gives people the right to do that?" She looked to Jae for more support and noted the young woman's sorrow. "Oh, Jae. I'm so sorry."

Jae's face was wet with tears. Her chin turned away in an attempt to hide her emotions. "You're so beautiful, Pia," she whispered, her voice trembling. "It breaks my heart to think that anyone would want to hurt you or make you feel less than just because of who you are."

A blush spread across Pia's face as she received the heartfelt compliment. "I've never been called beautiful before," she admitted. "I'm sure you face your own share of prejudice as well."

Ignoring the last statement, Jae tried to lighten the mood. "How about settling for ruggedly handsome?" she joked, mustering a small laugh. "You and me! We would make a great team. I have to fight prejudice for being Korean, and you for being gay. Maybe we should give it a shot."

Pia felt a pang of regret at the mention of being a loner. "I'm used to being alone, Jae," she confessed. "And maybe two people having a pity party isn't the best reason for a partnership."

Pia's words weighed heavily on her, causing a stone to form in her stomach. But before she could dwell on it further, Jae interrupted her thoughts. "Oh Crap! If we don't hurry, we'll be late," she exclaimed. Pia's head jerked up in surprise as she glanced at the clock. It read 3:20, giving them only forty minutes to make it to work on time and start their last shift before their much-needed days of Monday and Tuesday off

Chapter 9

The Whole Famn Damily

Just like any other regular day, at the Grill and Chill, customers came and went in various groups. There were loud groups, solitary travelers, crying babies, tired kids, and even long-established couples who seemed more interested in everyone else than each other, their eyes constantly monitoring the parking lot as a point of interest. Despite her watchful gaze, Pia never caught a glimpse of the young man with the fluorescent tipped hair.

"Maybe he'll visit again, right before we close," Jae remarked, interpreting Pia's disappointed expression as she passed by her.

"Maybe." She cast a wistful glance out of the expansive glass window. She wanted to ask Mr. Kramer about him. Had he ever seen the young man? But Mr. Kramer had not come in today.

Now, there would be a lull before the desert crowd made their way in, eager for mouthwatering pie, or a traveler realizing that stopping for nourishment would help them stay alert and secure. She observed an older model pickup truck, faded and off white, park in the side lot. The double cab held several adults.

Pia's tired eyes caught Jae's frustrated sigh, the exhaustion evident in the slump of her shoulders. She balanced a heavy tub filled with the last of the dishes, the clinking of plates and silverware echoing through the now spotless and arranged tables. A wave of despair washed over her as she scanned the empty restaurant, the dim lighting casting a melancholic glow. No rest for the weary today.

"It's okay. I got this. Take your break," Pia muttered, her voice tinged with weariness. Determined, she gathered four menus and four sets of tableware, the smooth surfaces cool against her fingertips. As she made her way towards a table, the pungent aroma of lingering food wafted through the air, a mix of grilled meat, coffee and freshly cleaned surfaces.

Just as she approached the table, the four individuals barged in, their entrance accompanied by the cacophony of their bickering and jostling. The tallest among them, with streaks of grey stubble on his chin, exuded an air of self-importance. A smug smirk played on his lips as he jerked his head towards the counter, catching Pia's gaze. The sound of his gum snapping punctuated the tense atmosphere, the whittled toothpick hanging precariously from his lip.

"Ah, I wanna sit in booth. My back's killing me," the young woman with long auburn hair whined.

"You'll sit where I tell yah." He slammed his haunches on a stool and placed both elbows on the counter with expectation.

Pia returned to the counter, skillfully arranging the dinnerware and menus in front of them. As she headed towards the water station, she couldn't help but overhear a boisterous laugh and a hushed comment from the younger man, who had a larger build and beady eyes set a bit too close together. He asked, "What's up with the Chink? When did they start allowing them in here?"

The tall young man sitting at the end also chuckled, although he didn't direct his gaze at anyone in particular.

Oh, boy! This was going to be a long service. Pia dared not look in Jae's direction. Get 'em fed. Get 'em out. Still, her hands trembled when she placed the ice water before them, the cubes dancing in the glasses. Her eyes slid furtively down the line, unexpectedly catching the gaze of the man at the end. Something about him seemed more humane and distinct from the rest of the group.

Placing their ticket on the wheel, she spun it inward to read the items to cook upon entering the kitchen. Pia shook her head surreptitiously toward Jae, her eyes dark with warning.

The four continued to banter inane comments amongst each other. The larger, older man in the group crunched his ice most obnoxiously while he thumbed through a fishing and wildlife magazine.

Pia repeatedly filled glasses, brought condiments, and fulfilled countless requests for extras, some of which she suspected were made just to see her run and wait on them. Pia managed her stress level until an excessively lengthy and loud comment caused her to shake like an earthquake.

"Why'ancha hire yourself some gooks like that one down there to help ya'all out?" He laughed. The young woman laughed as well, but more like a braying hee haw.

"Hey! You." Looking over at Jae. "You likee me? You wanna love me long time?" he jeered.

"Stop it, you idiot." The woman sitting next to him said crossly, but more out of jealousy than admonition, it sounded.

Pia defused the situation, "She doesn't speak English. Just waiting for the Greyhound Bus."

He continued to cackle to himself but found new satisfaction focusing on the remnants of his food.

Rubbing her belly in a seductive manner, the woman directed her gaze towards the man on the end. He avoided her coy glance and glanced up at the pie menu.

Feeling a false sense of security in that they were finished eating and the jackals would be leaving soon, Pia grabbed for the older man's plate, hoping to initiate the earliest departure possible. He pulled the plate back against her grasp and met her startled glance with a leer.

"You look for damn sure familiar."

Pia pursed her lips together and shrugged her shoulders. "Don't see how." She forced her voice to sound unaffected, causal like, but inside she was quaking like a tree in fall, braced for a winter storm.

His eyes were steeled hazel, and his mouth held a new toothpick twisting between his teeth. With venomed sarcasm, he said low and sure, "Yah. You like to bowl." He nodded with assurance and smirked at her paling form. "The dyke. From Branson, wasn't it?"

Pia stacked plates and turned to the swinging door with, "Nope. Not me."

The woman, with a voice high pitched now with her own sense of importance, contributed, "Oh yah. I remember her from court." She laughed, trying to get support from the man beside her that wiped his greasy mouth on a used napkin.

"Yah," the man sitting next to her said, jabbing his companion in the ribs with a stern look. "We read about that cunt in the papers. Right?"

The woman looked down, sullen.

The quiet man at the end spoke up, "Shut up you two. Come on, let's get rolling." He stood, signaling the big guy.

The signal that they were leaving should have been enough. She should have thought about Jae, sitting helpless in the back corner, and taken a moment to breathe, but she didn't. The next comment changed everyone's world, for better or worse, yet to be determined.

Jae slid under the table when the stack of dishes crashed on the back counter.

"Funny thing," Pia said with a razor edged voice. She turned and walked to the counter where the older man stood. She looked up at his glare, meeting him full force. "See, there's actually a difference between a dyke and a cunt."

The tooth pick dropped from his mouth to the counter.

"You see, a dyke wants to be the dominant, have a dick of her own. But a cunt is a straight female that likes to have dick or a dyke inside her ... you know, like your mother."

Pia was completely caught off guard by the unexpected left hook. His massive paw caught her square on the cheekbone and sent her flying backwards. "We shoulda just killed you in that robbery and called it good." The jerk roared, as she slid to the floor. He wiped his hand across his jeans. "No place in this world for lesbos."

Kelly screamed in hysteria, "I'm going to sue this damn restaurant if I lose this baby. Right Ryan?" She looked at him with a wild-eyed expression, spooning her hand to a near flat stomach. "DO something!"

The man referred to as Ryan reluctantly looked demur and cradled his arm around her, convincing her that an exit was best. She simpered in his embrace.

Pia's voice could be heard as she asked, "What did you say your name was?"

"My name is, none of your fucking business." He turned to leave.

The youngest of the three was pumped and had a wild glaze to his eyes. His grin was devilish as he added immaturely, "Yah, none of your business." He flicked a fork at Pia for good measure and looked at his brother in triumph. "Come on, Stan. Let's get out of here." The bells above the door jangled.

Stan reached over and smacked him in the head with frustration.

"What?"

His brother pushed him heavily out the door.

Pia smiled in triumph, tainted with fear. Stan. The name Willow used as his partner that night at the bowling alley.

Jae came running over as the group, now outside, ambled their way to their truck. Dismay filled Jae's face as she said, "My God! Are you all right? Of course, you're not all right. Why do people always say that-?"

"Jae-."

"I mean it's obvious you're not alright. His ring! It cut right into your skin-." She gasped.

"-Jae-."

"We should call the police. I mean we can't call the police. You could call the police-."

"JAE!"

Her head snapped up, fixing her gaze on Pia. Her eyes came into focus. They were big, like saucers. "What?" She said, shocked.

"Get me some ice."

CHAPTER 10

ESCAPE

With tentative attempts, she pressed the cold ice against the throbbing ache on the back of her head, where it had collided with the unforgiving counter. Jae, with delicate care, tenderly patted at the cut along her cheekbone. As Pia winced, a sharp intake of air filled her nostrils, mingling with the scent of antiseptic. The pain, vividly etched on her face.

Jae sat on her heels, her eyes fixated on Pia's injured cheek. The worry and concern etched on her face were palpable, almost tangible. Pia couldn't help but be captivated by the sight, her senses heightened. Just inches away, she studied the contours of Jae's face, tracing the curves and angles with her eyes. Her gaze wandered to the fullness of Jae's mouth, a sight that stirred a longing within her. She attempted to maintain an innocent facade, but the desire written across her face betrayed her true feelings, evoking a rush of conflicting emotions.

"Should we just close?"

"No. I can't miss Willow. He's got to help me. I don't want to deal with those yahoos anymore. Willow can get them busted as well. I'm sure the oaf that punched me was the Stan Willow was referring too. It's got to be." She sighed with exhaustion.

Jae exclaimed with excitement, "What are the chances? But thank God!" Jae hesitated, then blushed, "Is that true? You know, about dykes and cunts?"

Pia laughed, then winced at the pain. "Shit. I was just jerking their chain. Trying to get a reaction." She reached up and brushed Jae's shoulder. "You're cute."

Hesitation flickered in Jae's eyes as they gazed at Pia, a longing fueled by desire. Leaning in, the softness of her touch enveloped Pia's senses as Jae tenderly kissed the side of her mouth.

Pia swiftly turned, the sound of their exhales mingling in the air, and caught Jae's mouth with her own. Her lips, soft as silk, pressed against Pia's, creating a warm, electric sensation that sent a shiver through Pia's core. The embrace of their lips was both gentle and firm, creating a palpable quiver that resonated between them, like a melody playing in the stillness of the room. Pia gently sucked on Jae's top lip, the taste of anticipation lingering on their tongues, a pause, a request of sorts, before reigniting the kiss, a confirmation of their shared desire. As Pia pulled away, she noticed the blush blooming on Jae's face. The scent of innocence mixed with a lingering hint of lust hung in the air.

Her eyes returned to Pia's cut cheek.

"Don't pity me."

"I don't! I'm crazy about you."

"No, that won't work either. You don't know me."

"Yes, I do and what I see I really care about."

"I can't take care of you, Jae. I can't ... I'm a felon for God's sake!"

"So what! I'm a fugitive." She giggled.

"You're not a fugitive you didn't do anything wrong."

"Neither did you!"

Pia stood, separating them, dulling the moment of intimacy. Fear and doubt hung over her like a wet blanket damping the mood.

She stood as well, defiance written across her face, her eyes ablaze. "I don't need you to take care of me. I can be anywhere, do anything. But most importantly, I want to feel safe. I have that with you."

"Are you crazy?! You saw those maniacs tonight. Don't think they won't be back. Who knows what's going to happen now that they think I can identify them."

Jae hesitated briefly, then blurted, "Let's leave! Head to Wisconsin. I've got money!" She jabbered with fear in her voice.

"I can't leave the state, Jae. Terms of my probation, my invisible ball, and chain. But you ... you should go."

"Not without you."

Pia sighed with frustration and shook her head.

"I thought you cared about me."

"I do! It's just that-."

"What?"

"You, you're..."

"Too young? Too Korean? A virgin?"

"No!!! None of that matters! Wait, you're a virgin?"

"Pia! **We** make a good team. We found each other right when it mattered the most. I don't just need you, I want you. I love you."

"Don't! Don't love me." Pia stated with agitation. "You don't know what you're getting into. You have a whole life ahead of you-."

"Oh, seriously! You're only a few years older than me. We! We can have our whole lives ahead of us!" Jae came close to Pia, putting her arms around her waist, but Pia pushed her back.

"Why? Why can't we be together?"

Pia felt the knots of frustration and panic engorge her stomach. "I feel like I have to do more for you than I can do for myself." Pia continued, pained, "I'm afraid of disappointing you. Failing you. And sometimes you sound so ... so, desperate."

Jae stood frozen, her cheeks burning with embarrassment as tears streamed down her face. The room filled with a heavy silence, broken only by the faint sound of her choked sobs. The air carried a mix of tension and shame, making it difficult for her to breathe. Despite her anguish, her eyes glimmered with a defiant glare, determined not to let her emotions completely consume her. "Didn't see that coming." Jae grabbed her knapsack and slung it over her shoulder. "Well, don't worry about being put out. I was leaving tonight anyway."

"Jae, wait! Come on. I didn't mean I didn't want to be friends…"

"Unbelievable!" Jae continued to the side door and walked outside where the now cooled night air swallowed her small but voluptuous, retreating figure.

"Jae, you can't leave!" Pia called out as the door continued to close. "Where are you going?"

Frustrated, Jae grabbed the now melting ice bag and placed it on her hot cheek. She went to the kitchen to tidy up, feeling Jae just needed time to cool down.

She'll be back. Where would she go, anyway? Just to be sure, Pia went to the parking lot to see if she was sitting out there. Pia unlocked the door of the car in case she came by to wait.

Hours crept by until she could finally close. Disappointment engulfed her as only two strangers wandered in, with no sign of the young man with the white-tipped hair and brilliant blue eyes. Pia checked the parking lot twice, hoping to see Jae waiting for her, ready to apologize and move forward. But no sign of her lingered.

Pia felt melancholy, her mind filled with conflicting thoughts. She was crazy about the girl. But life now in a hotel room, working at a roadside diner? Not the romantic life she wanted to offer someone. She imagined Jae's life, a life of luxury and comfort, contrasting sharply with her own humble existence. The thought of offering Jae a life that fell short of her expectations made Pia's heart ache. Jae deserved the best. And yet, didn't she as well?

Pia cleaned the back kitchen area and swept and mopped the front. It had been so long doing this on her own she had forgotten how much work it was, and it took her much longer than she anticipated.

Pia switched off the interior lights one by one, feeling a tinge of regret as she locked the front door. Still no sign of Jae. As she made her way out through the back door, she took a moment to double-check that all the garbage bags were just outside before locking herself out.

With a heavy heart, she walked slowly, each step filled with a palpable sadness. The sight of the bags, burdened with memories, made her hesitate for a moment, hoping for a sound to echo from within the dumpster, as if Jae had magically returned to the place where it all started. But the silence enveloped her in a sigh of disappointment.

As Pia turned to leave, her eyes caught sight of an unfamiliar shape to her left, causing her to freeze in her tracks. The air seemed filled with a mix of anticipation and dread, her senses heightened. Her stomach sank, a knot tightening within her, as she instinctively knew that the prone figure before her was human. The sound of her own rapid heartbeat filled her ears. She reached down to touch the still bundle, her fingertips brushing against the fabric of the black hoodie, then recoiling.

A cry escaped her lips, a mixture of fear and anguish intertwining in the air. Her heart pounded in her chest, the thumping reverberating through her entire being. Wide blue eyes stared blankly at the star-filled sky with a milky glaze. The sight sent a shiver down her, a chilling realization settling in. Pia recoiled in horror, the feeling of dread intensifying. Her whole body trembling with a mix of disbelief and dread. He had returned tonight. But someone had taken his life in a cruel act of violence.

Oh, God! Jae!!! She suddenly remembered.

Pia sprinted desperately to the front parking lot, her heart pounding in her chest, her breath coming in ragged gasps as she fumbled with her keys, the cool metal slipping from her trembling hands. As she neared her vehicle, a wave of alarm washed over her. She took in the sight before her - the side driver's window, shattered and jagged, the other side window following suit. Her heart sank further as she noticed the devastating blows inflicted upon her car. The car bore the marks of a brutal attack, deep dents from what seemed like a forceful swing of a baseball bat, leaving their mark on every door and the hood. The windshield, now a chaotic maze of delicate cracks, resembled a fragile web spun by a malevolent spider.

Overwhelmed by the sensory assault, Pia couldn't help but feel a profound sense of violation. The scene before her eyes was not just a physical destruction, but a violation of her personal space, her sense of security shattered along with the glass.

As the realization settled in, Pia's heart raced, her pulse pounding in her ears. The warning hung in the air like a thick fog, chilling her to the core. She scanned the surroundings, her eyes darting nervously, searching for any sign of danger. The distant sound of traffic buzzed in the background, blending with the hushed whispers of the wind.

Who was responsible for all of this? The weight of the business card pressed against her fingertips, its texture rough and worn as her hand reached into her pocket. Odd that Jae's family had not contacted her directly. Would Jae do this? No way. Stan and his goons? More than likely. Was the patrolman, Jack Faber, mixed up in all this?

The thought of Jae's safety consumed her, filling her with a mix of determination and fear. With a trembling hand, she inserted the key into the ignition, feeling the cold metal against her skin. The engine roared to life; the sound echoing in her ears like a thunderclap. Pia's grip tightened on the steering wheel as she peeled out of the parking lot, the tires screeching against the asphalt. The adrenaline coursed through her veins, sending a surge of energy through her body. She could feel the wind whipping against her face, her hair flying wildly in the air. Every fiber of her being was focused on one thing — Finding Jae and keeping her safe.

Chapter 11

Cluster Muck City

With great anticipation, Pia threw open the hotel room door, only to have her heart sink with disappointment. The sight before her eyes was a letdown, as if someone had dimmed the lights and drained the colors from the room. The stillness of the air was punctuated only by the faint hum of the ceiling fan. A sense of emptiness engulfed her.

As Pia stood there, she noticed the silence. No sound of running water from the shower, which would have been Jae's first instinct upon returning. The thought of a shower suddenly appealed to Pia, as she became acutely aware of her own exhaustion. The idea of immersing herself in hot water promised not only physical relief but also a chance to gather her thoughts.

Taking a moment to secure her surroundings, Pia locked and double-bolted the door, creating a sense of safety amidst the uncertainty. She then shed her soiled clothes, feeling the heaviness of her blood-splattered t-shirt as she discarded it in the trash. The heat from the water enveloped her body, soothing her aching head and unknotting her tense muscles. The warm embrace of the water brought a temporary respite, allowing her mind to focus.

Jae, where could she be? The thought of having hurt Jae weighed heavily on Pia's heart, the image of sadness etched on that sweet woman's face haunting her thoughts. Pia racked her brain, desperate to think of possible explanations. There was no way Jae could have walked the arduous eight miles to the hotel. And she wasn't in the car... Could she have been taken? The idea sent a shiver through Pia, filling her mind with fear and disgust. The memories of the Branson police, their taunting voices, and illicit actions made it clear that she couldn't trust them, couldn't call for their help.

Think. Think.

Jae is a logical girl. She wouldn't just rashly run into the unknown without a plan. She sure as hell wouldn't just walk down the highway.

Logical. Of course. Pia smiled at her own stupidity. She turned off the water and dressed in haste. Pia took all their belongings and packed them, throwing the little they had in the back of the Explorer before speeding back to the diner. She glanced at her watch, 1:15 am.

As she entered the parking lot, Pia turned off her lights and glided to the edge of the building. The interior revealed darkness, with only the faint light of the coolers in the kitchen casting an eerie glow.

Pia checked the hiding spot and brought forth the spare key. She hoped this confirmed what she had been thinking, that Jae was already in the restaurant, had been the whole time, hiding, just waiting for Pia to leave. That would be most logical.

With stealth, she unlocked the front door with only the smallest of a click as the door bolt slid open. She reached up and held the bells as she pushed her body through the narrowed opening. Pia locked the door from the inside, leaving the key in the lock in case of a hasty departure. Her breath felt ragged, her stomach sick, in knots, praying for Jae to be in the kitchen, eating as always, not missing or worse yet, not dead beside Willow or in the dumpster.

She caught her breath and stopped in horror. It had never occurred to her to look **in** the dumpster. The thought of Jae gone from her life filled Pia with a depth of sadness she never thought possible. Sneaking be dammed, Pia burst through the swinging doors into the kitchen.

Pia laughed. "Jae-sung!"

Jae looked up in shock. A bite of peanut butter and jelly sandwich still in her mouth half chewed bulged in her cheek. The remnants of potato chips, a half drank strawberry milkshake, and an open can of sardines near her on the floor filled Pia with so much joy she thought she was going to burst.

"We gotta get out of here! Come on." Pia anxiously looked out to the parking lot over the swinging doors to make sure no one else was there.

"I'm still mad at you."

Pia noted the tear-stained cheeks with remorse but with insistence replied, "Jae, did you see or hear anything when you left?"

She looked up with sadness, her dulled response, as she was still lost in her own misery.

"Jae! Get your bag. I'm getting you out of here. Willow's dead."

Jae's turn to look shocked and grieved. "What?! How? Where?"

"Never mind all that. We don't have much time. I'm taking you to Wisconsin, or at least the bus station in Forsythe, then you can Greyhound it up North." She pulled Jae up by her arm and tossed the food remnants into the garbage. Pia strode to the counter. Using a pencil and an order tablet, she left a note for Mr. Kramer promising she would return in a

few days explaining everything. She
scratched out, re-wrote then scratched
out again the part about the dead body.
How could one possibly explain that on
17 lines of a 3 x 4 order pad? Hopefully
there would be a later time for that.

Pia reached out and took Jae's hand.
She followed obediently. Through the
dark, they crept to the front door,
looking with fear into the night. The
parking lot remained deserted.

Pia locked the door of the building
once they were out and edged her way to
the side of the building to make sure no
one lurked around the corner or behind
the Explorer. She thought twice about

replacing the spare key, putting in the front pocket of her jeans instead.

She motioned for Jae to continue towards her, the flickering utility pole light casting eerie shadows on their faces. She turned when Jae gasped in shock; the sound echoing through the still night. The sight of the car made her heart sink - mangled metal and shattered glass, a testament to the violence that had unfolded. Her expression twisted with dread and increased fear, Jae's eyes widening as she took in the scene.

"Get in!" Pia hissed urgently, her voice barely audible above the distant hum of traffic.

Jae dashed to the passenger side, her footsteps sounding hurried on the pavement. Pia scanned the surroundings, her heart pounding in her chest, her palms slick with nervous sweat. She checked the back seat, the leather cold under her trembling hands, and tossed Jae's backpack inside. This time, of all times, the vehicle stuttered to start, the engine sputtering like a dying breath. Panic clawed at Pia's throat, her vision darting wildly in all directions, searching for any sign of danger emerging from the darkness. The engine finally caught, its growl breaking the silence, and Pia roared over the uneven sidewalk, the vibrations reverberating through the car, as she swerved onto the highway, turning right towards Mildred.

As they journeyed for miles, a heavy blanket of silence enveloped them, broken only by the occasional hum of the engine. Pia's eyes darted to the rearview mirror, searching for any glimmer of headlights piercing through the darkness. The rural landscape, devoid of streetlights, offered a cloak of secrecy, and they pressed on, immersed in the comforting embrace of the velvety night.

"Who did this to our car? Was it those guys?"

Pia smiled at the term *our car*. With focus, she said bitterly, "I honestly don't know. I think it might have been your family though." She looked at Jae to study her response.

Jae didn't look as surprised or worried as Pia would have expected. "Why would you think that? Not that they're not capable of it or anything."

Pia pulled the business card with the gold dragon emblem from her front shirt pocket and handed it to Jae. "This was in the front seat of the car."

"Why didn't you tell me?"

Pia shrugged. "I didn't want to worry you."

"What happened to Willow?"

Pia explained what she knew and what she speculated. "I have a feeling the next time I see the Groods, it won't be for coffee. But Willow's body? Left where it was...? That was a message just for me."

"How so?"

"They know I know. If I call the cops now and try to explain everything it'll look like I got vengeful towards Willow for getting me locked up and a fight ensued." She pointed to her cheek. "They'll just think I killed him. It won't matter if I say it was an accident or on purpose, or that I'm innocent." Pia looked at Jae to see if this was all sinking in. "I'm on parole. They'll send me back to finish my original 10 year sentence."

"But what about the patrol man-?"

"What about him? Do you think it was just coincidence he was there that night? Them, your family? Faber might be mixed up in all this too. I just don't know. The way that all this is coming together is just plain crazy." She spoke with an apologetic tone, "I even doubted you."

Jae tilted her head toward Pia and asked with curiosity, "Do you think I'm part of this?"

Pia shook her head in frustration. "I'm beside myself with fear. I just know I have to keep you safe."

Jae looked ahead through the unyielding of the dark night, adjusting her sight through the cracks in the windshield. "I can imagine how scary this all is. I do have something to tell you."

A loud pop sounded, and the car slowed to a halt. The silence from the engine gave Pia a hollow feeling in the pit of her stomach.

"Oh dear God! Betsy! You can't quite on us now!" She slammed her palm on the steering wheel for effect. The car coasted to a stop.

"Oh, no!"

Through the dense haze of the headlights, Pia could make out the faint outline of worn tracks in the grass.

"Help me push the car into the bushes over there!"

Putting the car in neutral, Pia pushed and steered the vehicle through the faded tracks, while Jae pushed from behind. The car picked up some speed as it went over the shoulder and rolled down to the soggy bottom area.

"It's too far. Now what?"

"No, it's perfect, just a few more feet, and we can hide it in the dogwood shrub. No one will see it from the road. We can hang out here until we figure out what to do."

"Good, because I have a dire need to use the bathroom right about now."

Pia looked up sharply. "What did you say?"

"I said, I had a dire need..."

Pia pointed to the brush where the lights to the car still held shadow play to the area. "Toilet paper is in the glove box. I'll wait here." She looked disconcerted.

After they made sure the tail end couldn't be seen from the road, the women climbed into the back like they had done so many nights before and laid side by side to contemplate their next move.

"I'm pretty sure this car is going to need a major repair. I won't be able to get it going. I was hoping to use the dark of night to at least get you to Forsythe without being pulled over for the broken windshield, but that's out. We can't hitchhike, God knows whose driving along this county road and I don't want to be seen by that highway patrolman. Just not sure about him yet."

Jae was silent.

Pia sighed with ire. "You put this on the front seat of the car. Didn't you?" She flicked the business card with the Gold Dragon emblem where it landed on Jae's chest.

Jae held a pout of guilt on her face.

"I was going to tell-."

"Do you know how worried I was? How scared I was for both if us? Why would you do that!?"

"I had to make sure."

"Sure of what?"

"Of us! Our friendship. I was afraid you might turn me in ... for the money."

"Unbelievable! You came to me, remember?"

"That's not how I remember it."

"However it went down, I really resent what you did."

"I'm sorry. But I had to know if you were in it for the money. You don't understand how frightened I am, of what my father is capable of."

"So you just carry around business cards to see how people react ... or don't react?"

"No. That one is my brothers. Each of us have a different colored dragon. His is gold, mine is white and my older brother's is red."

"And your father?"

"Black."

"Do you doubt me, even now?"

"No. No I don't. My brother won't tell my family where I am-."

"You mean, he knows?"

"Yes. He left this card in the passenger seat the day after you found me. He was telling me he knows where I am and wanted me to reach out."

"Did you?"

"No. My fathers' import/export business is legit, but the man he arranged me with is a crooked politician. I have no desire to return. How did you know I put this in the car for you to find?"

"Two things, one, no one says dire, and that's the second time in a week I heard it, 2nd you locked the door after you put it in the car. You're OCD. No one who broke in would then lock the door." She chuckled despite herself.

They were silent for some time, letting the new information sink in and allowing Pia's anger to subside. Finally, as the chill of the night settled in, Pia relented. "Let's get you out of here."

"Why can't we stay together?"

"Jae, I'm a felon, I can't leave the state, I have to follow the conditions of my probation and I can't even vote. I mean, honestly."

"What if we have proof you were innocent?"

"I'm not sure how we could do that now with Willow dead. Besides, the next time we're together, I'm sure they'll do more than punch me."

Jae cried quietly in frustration and sadness. The whole thing seemed so hopeless. Seeking solace, Jae slowly made her way towards Pia's shoulder, feeling the comforting warmth of her embrace as she nestled into her side.

Pia readily pulled her into her side embrace, spontaneously kissing the top of her head. "Won't do us any good if either of us ends up dead."

Jae's hand glided along Pia's neck, its gentle touch sending a tingling sensation down her spine. Pia couldn't help but quiver with desire, feeling the electric pulse in the pit of her stomach. As their embrace tightened, the softness of Pia's breasts pressed against Jae's chest, creating a warm and tantalizing sensation.

With a slight tilt of her head, Jae tenderly locked her lips on Pia's chin, her kiss filled with tenderness and longing. Jae's leg delicately wrapped over Pia's abdomen, an enticing invitation that ignited a deep and primal yearning to connect their souls. Their bodies intertwined.

After a time, Pia gently released their passionate embrace, her fingers delicately combing through Jae's hair. As she looked into Jae's eyes with tenderness, the soft scent of their surroundings filled her nostrils. With a slight tug at Jae's jacket, it slid off her shoulder, revealing a glimpse of smooth skin. In a moment of shared desire, they instinctively moved apart, their hands eagerly fumbling with their clothing, craving the sensation of bare, quivering flesh. Pia, feeling a surge of longing, pulled Jae to her knees, their bodies pressing chest to chest, their faces intimately close. With every feather-light kiss, Pia brushed softly against Jae's creamy shoulders. She savored the velvety touch. Jae, her anticipation growing, hesitantly placed her hands on Pia's shoulders, her breath mingling, warm and electric against Pia's neck.

Pia's firm hands glided along Jae's rib cage, her fingertips lightly brushing the edge of her breasts. The intense sound of their breaths mingled in the air, punctuated by small gasps escaping from Jae's lips. As the sensations intensified, Jae's hands rose to Pia's hardened nipples, pinching them delicately. A sweet scent of arousal filled the car, blending with the subtle fragrance of their skin. Pia, feeling a surge of pleasure, placed her hand beneath Jae's shoulder blade and nestled her head against Jae's neck, planting tender kisses along the sensitive skin behind her ear.

With a teasing touch that tauntingly glided downward, Pia's fingertips grazed the edge of Jae's labia, eliciting a shiver of anticipation. "My God, you're so wet," she whispered, as her fingers entered Jae, her voice filled with desire.

Jae shuddered with ecstasy at Pia's delight. The tantalizing sensation of Pia's fingertips touching her clit caused her butt to dip down, right into Pia's other hand. The space echoed with Jae's breathless moans, growing louder with each skillful stroke of Pia's longest finger against her velvety folds. A tingling sensation radiated from her swollen clit, intensifying as Pia expertly applied pressure. The sound of their passionate encounter harmonized with the rhythm of their breathing, creating a symphony of desire. Pia's other hand, entwined in Jae's hair, tugged back firmly, igniting a mix of pleasure and pain. Her lips, warm and eager, found solace on Jae's small breast, sucking hungrily as her other hand skillfully continued to explore every fold of Jae's quivering velvet.

Jae's orgasm erupted from her in a fiery cry that echoed over and over as her undulating waves of passion swept through her. She fainted back, overcome with the sensation. Pia pulled her lightly to her. She kissed Jae's mouth with passion over and over with feather kisses, sucking her bottom lip with a tantalizing pull while she slowly ever so slowly reduced the touch of her palm, all four fingers in a firm swirl, releasing in reluctance.

Jae's arms hung limp while Pia kissed her on the cheeks, her forehead, her neck, and chest. Minutes later, Jae felt like she was catching her breath.

"Feel good?"

"My God! Yes, that was amazing!" Her eyes met Pia's with tenderness and she hesitatingly brought her hand to Pia's warmth.

Placing two fingertips on Pia's clit, she massaged with soft pressure. Pia engaged Jae with a deep kiss. Their tongues touching, tasting, igniting passion again. Jae's body trembled uncontrollably. Pia moaned with the anticipation of their love making bringing an unquenchable fire to light again. She smiled at Jae's desire to please her and after a time brought Jae's hand to her heart.

"You're not able to come?"

"Not tonight. I will though. I'll teach you." She kissed Jae, tasting her mouth with urgency, touching her tongue to hers. "But right now, I want to taste you, put you inside me." Pia leaned Jae back, and with one quick motion, lifted her legs around her neck. She wasted no time pushing her mouth into Jae's lower lips, sucking the juices and lapping firmly against the sensitive cherry that quivered under Pia's tongue.

Jae gasped and thrust her hips up. She moaned deeply. Pia reached her hands up to Jae's breasts and cupped them, using a firm grasp. Pia increased the pressure on her clit, using her lips to suck. Jae began to buck. She squeezed Jae's pebble hard nipples to the point of pain but continued a slow steady French kiss style of engagement with her sex. Jae's smell was intoxicating, and Pia moaned deeply with excitement. Jae cried aloud over and over, her hips thrusting with the same pace as her lustful moans. Pia raised her off the floor of the car and sucked her hard as she placed two fingers inside Jae's throbbing wetness.

Jae experienced an earthquake wave of pleasure that nearly made her faint. The waves undulated through her, in her, around her, and left her breathless and emotional. Jae cried with the enormity of pleasure and euphoria. She pulled at Pia's head to release her grip from her clit as the pleasure became too intense.

Pia wiped her mouth on Jae's soft belly as she flowed upwards, chest to chest, heart to heart, to hold her while she relaxed through her afterglow.

They laid quiet, together for some time. Pia stroking her back and hair while Jae rested on her chest.

"Do you really think your dad will stop looking when you turn 18 next month?" She finally asked.

"He will when he finds out I'm gay."

"What do you mean?"

"If I embarrass him that would be worse than just running away. We can contact my brother and tell him why I ran, even though that's only part of it. My dad would rather be a little frustrated about an unruly, bottom of the rung daughter who ran away, than to publicly announce I'm gay and totally unavailable in the marriage market. That would affect his standing in the public business world and in his mind cause great shame."

Pia contemplated what she said. After a few minutes, Pia seemed energized. "Come one. Let's head back to the café."

"Why?"

"We're going to tell Mr. Kramer everything." She hesitated. "Well, not everything." Pia waved at Jae's naked form with an impish grin. "You know what I mean."

“No. I really don’t.”

Chapter   12

Brokeback or Bust

"Come on! We'll use the Geo to make the run, then ditch the car." Stan looked up at the group to make sure they were clear on the plan. "Ryan, you stay here. We should be back by daylight."

"Aw, Stan! Come on. I could use a break too. I could stay at the diner in case the Greyhound comes early." He pleaded.

Stan's eyes narrowed with suspicion, then irritability. "Nah. Waylen and I will take the run to Forsyth. We don't have cash coming tonight anyways."

This statement perplexed Ryan. He was sure a cash drop at the Grill & Chill was coming through the Greyhound bus tonight. The boys had only been back an hour or so from an earlier run in which Ryan had also not been included, and now they were leaving again. Leaving him with Kelly. He was worried they were doubting his loyalty.

*   *   *

The women grabbed a few basic essentials from the car and began the long walk back to Hollister.

"We have to get back before light. I'm not sure how this is going to work, its already quarter to four."

Jae fumbled with her pack. "We could call Mr. Kramer and ask for a ride."

Pia stood dumbfounded. "You've got a phone?! Now, you tell me you have a phone?!! That would have been good information to have, oh, I don't know, a month ago."

Jae looked sheepish. "I have trust issues."

Pia called Mr. Kramer, but of course at this hour it went straight to voicemail. They continued their plight, moving furtively along the roadside ditch until they could get to another mile marker and call Kramer again, hoping he would answer before the sunrise exposed them to unknown traffic.

A few more miles along their trek and the glow of headlights traveling their way marked a car coming. Fear besieged the pair and as the car approached the women, they shrank into the tall grass in the ditch beside the road. Jae gasped as they saw Willow's green Metro racing by at a high speed.

*　　　*　　　*

"The first pull out you see, drive in. Cut the lights."

Waylen pulled the metro into a faded, worn set of tire tracks. They glided just a few feet down.

"I'll be damned. Check it out."

The fugitive men spotted, through their squinted eyes, an old abandoned vehicle in the brush.

"I got an idea. Help me grab the cash."

Pia called Mr. Kramer again and left another message.

"Uh oh. Trouble."

Pia looked up at a set of flashing lights blinking their ominous warning, surely meant for the Geo but coming their way.

No time to run ahead or behind to avoid being detected. The girls dove into weeds again and pressed their bodies close to the earth as the Highway Patrolman whizzed by.

Using the tip Ryan had provided him, Jack Faber was waiting for the pair at the Chill & Grill. The car turned left towards Mildred, though, instead of going straight to Branson. Now driving several miles without sight of the vehicle, Jack realized they must have pulled over and hid. But as he drove at top speed back along the highway, he could see the small form of the vehicle traveling at even greater speed back toward Hollister. They must have pulled over, hid and tried to back track without him noticing.

Pushing the cruiser at top speed, Jack, with great skill, closed in upon the Geo and blurted the sirens. The compact car was in the lead, but not a match for the cruiser.

The Geo slowly slowed down and pulled to the right of the road, turning off their brights.

Pia tried not to gasp as she saw Faber, the highway patrolman from the café, walk to the side window of the Metro.

Jack commanded the reticent driver, Stan, from the front seat. He had the driver put his hands on the front grill while he searched him for weapons. No one noticed the trunk open and close as a second fugitive exited the car.

"Stay right here. I have probable cause to search your vehicle."

"Go right ahead." He said with a smirk.

Jack rapidly opened the back door of the vehicle, then the trunk, always keeping vigil over the con leaning on the hood. He frowned in disappointment.

"Well, guess I got you on speeding, tonight." He walked up to Stan, placing his flashlight beam in Stan's eyes.

"Probably get me for no insurance or registration as well."

Jack was clearly frustrated, but he rescinded to pull out his ticket book when the sound of an electric current filled the air, then the smell of burning flesh, before he dropped to the ground.

"Let's get this idiot in the car. Tie him up, Waylen." The men proceeded to subdue the patrolman with another zap of the Taser and lifted him with great difficulty into the Geo Metro and sped off.

*   *   *

As the car screeched away, leaving the smell of gas fumes and burnt rubber in their nostrils, Pia looked furtively over her shoulder to make sure Jae was okay. She was amazed and in awe that not only was she doing ok, but she was video-taping the entire conversation that had taken place, including the tazing of the highway patrolman.

"I guess he wasn't in on it," said Pia after they pulled away, officer in the trunk.

"What now? Keep running, hoping Kramer answers his phone?"

"Heck no! We got wheels, complete with lights and sirens." Pia grinned as she pointed toward the police cruiser. "Hop in!"

*   *   *

"Well, lookee here! Man, you guys did good. How'd yah get 'em the car?"

Waylen looked so pleased with himself. "Ryan, it was like taking candy from a baby." He snickered. The patrolman winced at the added back hand Waylen delivered.

Stan said with a sour tone, "He thought he was real smart pulling me over. But we had already hid the drugs and the money in some old, abandoned car we found along the highway, then headed back. Worst he coulda got us for was speeding and no insurance. Used the stun gun we got that kid with to subdue him."

Ryan was curious. "Where is that kid, anyway?"

He twirled the toothpick in his mouth, "Thought we told yah. We roughed him up a bit, after we had him bash in that waitress's car. Testing him a little. He was deader than a door nail after he hit his head on the dumpster."

He turned his attention to finish his sentence while he looked at Jack. "We weren't going to keep him around anyways."

"You killed Willow?"

"Oh, come on now. Don't get all soft and squishy about it. You knew he was the leak." Waylen jerked his thumb toward the patrolman. "I confirmed it the night we saw this cupcake sitting at the diner with him and the waitress, getting all cozy like."

Stan sternly added, "We can't have no loose ends. Let's beat the holy living shit out of this guy and find out what else he knows before we bury him."

Ryan's eyes widened. Before he could respond, the door burst open and Kelly entered, all breathless. "The preacher's here. Says he wants to talk to yah." Her eyes reflected panic as she glanced at the prisoner, tied and gagged in the chair.

"Why's *he* here? Dang it all!" Stan grimaced and pushed his way past Ryan and Waylen to get to the door. "Come on, Waylen. I don't want him to know we didn't finish the run. Ryan, you stay here and keep an eye on this bastard. I'll be bringing the chainsaw." He grinned wide.

Ryan nodded and shut the door behind them. Kelly stood by, all nervous like. Ryan tried to calm her. "Go on

now. Pack a bag like I told yah. Then
skip on out to the woods by the stream
till I come get yah." He kissed her on the
forehead for good measure and she
nodded her head, still struck by the sight
of the subdued man in the chair.

Ryan guided her to the door with his
hand on her elbow. "Everything's going
to be alright. Just do like I said. Don't
come out of the woods, till I call for
yah."

"Okay. Okay," she responded
nervously as she left.

Ryan closed the door and peeked out
of the small curtained window. No sign

of anyone else, except Kelly's jiggling form sneaking to her cabin.

"Pack a bag?"

"Well, I had to give her some hope. I told her if the shit was going to hit the fan that this would be our plan, so we could sneak off and get married." He walked to Jack and stroked his forehead, careful to miss the welt. "How in the hell did they catch you?"

Jack let out a big sigh. "I thought I had it in the bag. Plus, I only saw one of them in the car when I was in pursuit."

"Too bad. This would have all been over if you would have caught them with the stash. Now what?" He asked, as he untied Jack from his restraints.

"I'm going to get out of this line of work, so we can be together. Be safe."

Ryan reached up and kissed him with tenderness, "You don't have to change your line of work. I know you love it. We just need to get the fuck out of Missouri where I don't hear banjos playing in the background like some scene out of a, what did you call it? Deliverance movie?"

"You're sexy when you're mad."

"Now is not the time."

"I'm glad you can find the humor in this, but I'm sure you caught the fact that once the preacher is gone, I'm next." Jack stood and held Ryan in a bear hug. "You have to stay here, Ryan. I'll go get SWAT and end this. You'll be arrested with them so your cover isn't blown."

"How am I going to explain that?"

"I'm going to have to hit you, pretty hard. Make it look like we struggled. You'll spend hours looking for me in the brush. That will give enough time for the Feds to get here." Jack threw the chair around the room until it broke and dumped odds and ends around on the floor. "Still got the phones charged out at the Cottonwood snag?"

"Um, yah." He added tentatively, "How hard?"

"What?" He answered Ryan with distraction. "Like, stiff cock in the morning hard, but inside of an iceberg."

He shook his head with dread. "That's pretty hard. Can you-?"

The hit came from left field. Ryan didn't even have a chance to duck. He was out cold.

*   *   *

"Well, that's quite a story. I wish I would have let you in on a few things.

But, that family is dangerous. I didn't want you to have no part of that." Mr. Kramer blew on his milky coffee while he digested all that Pia and Jae had told him. "I'll get a tow truck to get your vehicle up to Forsythe and get the windows and the engine fixed. You can pay me back later."

"Thank you so much, Mr. Kramer. I will pay you back, I swear."

Jae swallowed her hash browns mixed with sausage gravy before she spoke. "Mr. Kramer if you don't mind me asking. How did you get mixed up in all this?"

He sighed with regret. "I've been here so long, know so much about so many people. We all have secrets. I should have known sooner or later mine would catch up with me." He dug into his sausage links the first shift cook had made for him, along with orange and cinnamon coated French toast. "The Butlers asked me a few years ago to use the diner as a stash. I said no. They knew about my relationship with the preacher's daughter and threatened to expose me."

Jae wrinkled her nose in concern. "So, was this like something that happened a year or so ago?"

"Oh, God no. Heck I was 19 and she was 16. We were in love." He looked soft in the dimmed light of the café as he reminisced. The sun, not quite awake, only peeked through the blinds, half drawn on the windows. "But the Butlers said they had pictures of some sort. Even now, if the preacher knew... well it could be bad."

"But we know that highway patrolman wasn't in on it. If we find him, you can get all that straight!"

"You don't know the old ways here, Pia. If you fight back, try to go against the fold, you could end up in the deepest part of the woods or alongside of the highway."

Mr. Kramer continued. "No. I'll just keep my back up and deny this spot as a drug run. At least as long as I own it. Which might not be too much longer. But anyway, to help you, send that video to my phone. Leave the police cruiser here and I'll get that evidence where it needs to go."

While thanking him profusely, Kramer pointed an aged finger to the window where the rumpled figure of Jack, the highway patrolman, was weaving his way to the entrance. The 18-wheeler that assisted with the human drop off made a hasty exit from the side of the road.

"Go on. Take the keys to my Caddie. Don't come back till I tell you it's safe. GO!" He roared.

Chapter   13

Cha' Ching

Pia pushed open the bathroom door with sweet anticipation. Wisps of steam enveloped her, obscuring her vision. She squinted, straining to make out the silhouette of Jae amidst the swirling mist. The sound of cascading water filled her ears, punctuated by the rhythmic patter of droplets drumming on the tiled floor. With haste, Pia unbuttoned her outer shirt, the fabric rustling against her fingertips. The scent of warm, humid air mixed with the faint aroma of jasmine-scented soap wafted through her nose, arousing her senses. With a gentle tug, she tore off her tank top; the fabric sliding smooth against her skin. The metallic clank of her belt buckle hitting the floor reverberated in the steam-filled room, blending with the sound of the shower. Jae leaned her head back from the shower wall, turning to face Pia, her eyes gleaming with desire. A smile of anticipation played on her lips as their gazes locked in an electric connection.

As she approached Jae, Pia's fingers gently brushed the back of her shoulders, sending shivers through Jae's body. Her hands explored every inch of Jae's body, gliding over her slick skin. Pia's fingertips traced the curves of Jae's small breasts, feeling the softness beneath her touch.

The sensation sent waves of pleasure coursing through both of them.

Her soft gasps enticed Pia to utter her own moan of pleasure. Pia pressed her face into the crook of Jae's neck, inhaling the sweet scent of her sweat. Her fingertips brushed against Jae's hardened, thick nipples, the slickness of the skin under her touch sending quivers of desire through her. Slowly, she slid her hands along Jae's soapy waist, feeling the tremble of her on Pia's fingertips. The room filled with hushed moans that escaped Jae's lips, blending with the pounding of the water.

Pia's hands continued their journey, sliding down Jae's sides, the smoothness of her skin accentuated by the steam that enveloped them made her quiver. She reached Jae's full hips. With a gentle squeeze, Pia cupped Jae's plump butt, relishing in its voluptuousness. As their bodies moved in sync, the heat of the steam intensified, wrapping around them like a warm embrace. Pia leaned forward, her lips barely grazing Jae's shoulders in feather-light kisses. Her breath was husky with anticipation, inhaling the delicate scent of her skin mixed with the intoxicating jasmine soap.

In this moment of urgency and desire, their bodies turned and shifted, the urgency palpable as their hands and lips found their mark. With a gentle

pressure, Pia's hands glided back over
Jae's full hips. The sensation of their
curves beneath her palms was
intoxicating. With a light, teasing
squeeze, she brought her hands back to
cup Jae's full butt, savoring the firmness
beneath her touch. Pia's tongue traced a
path along Jae's shoulders, the taste of
her skin mingling with the steam and hot
mist that enveloped them made her ache
with desire. Pia gently tilted Jae's chin
up, their eyes locking in a determined
gaze. The air was filled with anticipation,
as the sound of their breaths was a lustful
harmony. When their lips met again, a
soft, velvety sensation spread, igniting a
fiery longing deep within their bodies.
The taste of desire lingered in the air,

mingling with the scent of passion, as they hungrily sought for more.

*　　　*　　　*

Later, as they lay on the hood of the Caddie and watched clouds scurry overhead, they held hands and shivered a bit, feeling the caress of the wind over their blanketed bodies.

Pia spoke softly, expressing her desires. "I wish I could promise you a life, Jae. You deserve to have everything."

Jae, deep in thought, still held a pink glow of their lovemaking on her face. She recalled a quote by Mark Twain and shared it with Pia, "You know, Mark Twain once said that you'll be more disappointed by the things you didn't do than the things you did. Sometimes, you have to sail away from the safety of the harbor."

Pia sighed, acknowledging the truth in those words, but also expressing her concerns. "Easier said than done. I can't vote, I can't own a gun. I'm not sure if I can protect you the way I'd like to. I don't want to diminish your chances of having a full life. You deserve everything, Jae."

"You underestimate me and my part in all of this." She snuggled closer and pulled the blanket tighter around them. "Let's give this a try. I don't have any expectations. I just know when I'm with you I'm really happy."

She holds Jae, who is so soft and full, into her side embrace. "I love the shape of you, next to me," she whispers, feeling a warmth spread through her heart.

Pia lay in silence for some time, her gaze fixed on the horizon. As she contemplated the moment, a mix of emotions washed over her - gratitude for having Jae by her side, but also a deep-seated worry about the uncertainties that lie ahead. She knows Jae doesn't understand the whispers floating through the town like a wildfire, their power growing with each passing moment. These rumors about them, like tendrils of smoke, intertwine with their lives, threatening to unravel the fragile bond they share.

Finally she spoke with vulnerability to Jae. "The whispers of our future can be powerful. Like me staying here and fixing up Kramer's place, owning it someday. We could run it together you and me. Or I could see about interstate compact and move my parole to Wisconsin. You could do your schooling there if you wanted." She hesitated, then spoke with conviction. "I really love you, Jae."

Pia waited in the stillness for Jae's response. Pia looked down to see Jae's closed eyes. Her regular breathing let her know, Jae probably had not heard a word of her whispered dreams or sincere words of commitment through her slumbered state.

I heard a whisper

It called out your name.

The sound was a melody

Its source was purity, no tone of shame.

Whispers can harm us, define how we feel.

Whispers define us, our dignity they steal.

Our whisper is infinity. Together we rise.

For the whisper of love conjoins us, our truth

needs no disguise.

I heard a whisper. I called out your name.

I'm ready to join you, this union called us,

two Soul's eternal flame.

*   *   *

"If only there was a way to prove my innocence. But with Willow dead, there's no one to corroborate my story now."

The following morning had arrived, and they were dressing in warmer attire for the day. Mr. Kramer had phoned earlier that morning and instructed the women to make their way back. He had some news to share, assuring them it was now safe to return.

As the girls arrived at the diner, their eyes were immediately drawn to a black SUV that sat in the parking lot. Pia couldn't help but feel a pit in her stomach.

"Stay here Jae, until I check it out. Keep the keys just in case."

Jae nodded, her brows furrowed with worry, her face etched with lines of concern.

When Pia stepped into the bustling diner, a cacophony of clinking silverware and lively chatter filled the air. The aroma of sizzling bacon and freshly brewed coffee wafted through the space, mingling with the faint scent of pancake syrup. As her eyes scanned the room, they landed in a corner booth, where Jack, the highway patrolman, sat with

Mr. Kramer. A sense of fear washed over her when she noticed seated beside him was Ryan, the sarcastic addition of the Butlers, who had visited a few days earlier.

Before she could turn and make a hasty exit, Mr. Kramer caught sight of her and gestured for her to join them. She paused, unsure of what to do.

"Pia! It's okay." He called out. He mouthed without saying aloud, "They're undercover cops."

Pia sighed in relief. She nodded and rushed out to signal the 'all clear' to Jae.

Pia noticed the expression of fear on Jae's face, prompting her to approach the side window. She wanted to reassure Jae that both Jack and Ryan were inside conversing with Kramer. "By now, he has shown them the video, so they should know that they can rely on us. I'm certain it will strengthen our case. What's the matter?"

"I think I know a way to help you too."

Pia looked confused

"I was waiting for a good time," Jae said as she opened a video on her phone. She showed Pia a clip that she had recorded on the night when the Butlers were causing trouble at the diner and admitting their involvement in the Branson hold-up.

Pia's face clouded. "You were going to tell me at a good time? Like when? Christmas?" Pia felt resentment. "This knowledge really could have helped me relax, you know!"

Her bottom lipped trembled. "I love you so much. I'm okay with whatever happens to me. I want you to be free."

"What do you mean, whatever happens?"

"When all this comes out, my dad will read about this in the papers or hear about it on the news. I'll be brought in. You don't know my father and the pull he has."

Pia allowed her anger to dissipate. She understood why Jae hesitated revealing the video. Speaking with unwavering determination, she said, "When we hand this over, let's include your anonymity in the deal. Jack truly needs this information, and so do the rest of us. For me, for Kramer, for Willow. And for everyone else who has endured suffering at their hands." Carefully, she pulled Jae out of the car and held her tenderly. "I'll keep you safe, Jae. Just another month. We can make it through."

"We?"

"Yes, we!" Pia whispered, her voice filled with determination as she gently tilted Jae's chin upwards, their eyes locking in a moment of unwavering resolve. The air was electric with anticipation, as the soft touch of their lips grew into a passionate, lingering kiss.

. The sensation sent a tremor of pleasure through them, igniting a fiery longing that pulsed through their bodies, leaving them yearning for more.

"Ready?" Pia asked breathlessly.

Jae nodded.

"Who's this?" The highway patrolman asked Pia when she came back in.

Pia hesitated, "My ... girlfriend."

Jae pulls out her phone and shows video of the Butler confession on her phone. "I was afraid to come forward with it because we didn't know if this cop was working for my dad, and if this gets to the newspaper and I'm linked to it ... well, my dad will find me. Plus, I wasn't sure about Pia until..., well, I just wasn't sure" She added breathlessly, "Can you help us?"

"First of all. I'd like to apologize," said Ryan. He looked sincere as he explained to the group about his undercover work with a sting operation with several groups of people, the Butlers being only one of them. "I never meant any of those awful things that were said. But yes! We can help you. SWAT arrested all those connected to this drug ring running through three counties."

The group spent some time discussing the sequence of events and the remarkable way in which they all came together. Jack assured the ladies he would work on expunging Pia's record and keeping Jae out of the picture.

Ryan added, "And about your car. Again, I'm very sorry. Part of keeping my cover, but I'll find a way to make it up to you, I swear!"

*   *   *

Two days later, the Explorer arrived at the diner with new tires, new windows, a new fan belt and a nice fat bill of $3800.

"I'll work as long as I need to Mr. Kramer, to pay you back."

"I know you will, Pia. I'm just glad things are returning to normal. Feeling safe. You know?"

"Yes! It's an amazing feeling to know I might be completely free soon! Such a good feeling." They turned to the sound of a car horn beeping. Pia waved and smiled at Jae, grinning from ear to ear sitting in the front seat of the still dinged up Explorer. Pia didn't have the heart to tell her there was no way she could afford to go to Wisconsin now.

"I'm going to check out these new tires you put on Betsy!" She thanked Mr. Kramer again and headed out the door with excitement.

As she skipped out of the restaurant, Mr. Kramer stopped to answer the phone. He put the caller on hold to call out to Pia. "Oh, I forgot to tell you. I found a lawyer we can use!" The door had closed just enough to block his words against the customers' chatter inside and the traffic outside. He put the opaque business card with the emblem of a black dragon back in his billfold. "Plenty of time to talk about it later," he conceded.

Once the girls arrived back at the hotel, they wasted no time in preparing for a much needed day trip to Forsythe. While Jae prepared to throw in her overnight bag, she called out to Pia, curious about the multitude of boxes occupying the back of the Explorer. "What's with all these boxes in the back of the Explorer?"

Pia approached, tossing her bag into the mix, along with some sleeping bags, just in case. She added a smile as she did so. Her smile transformed into a look of shock when Jae opened one of the boxes. The container had stacks of cash filled to the brim.

Both women stood stunned. They could hardly breathe.

"Finders keepers." Said Pia, with no shame.

"No shit."

"The Butler's blunders have struck again." With trepidation she asked, "What about the drugs?"

Jae pulled open box after box. Sitting back on her heels, a glistening sweat on her brow, she heaved a sigh. "No drugs. Just the cash." Jae giggled until tears streamed from her eyes.

*   *   *

Mr. Kramer was deeply grateful for the money that the women presented to him. Pia lied it was a gift from her grandfather, intended as a way to repay him for all the trouble he had gone through and to express their gratitude for all his efforts. She explained she had just been able to get in touch with him and this was money he had saved for her. Additionally, they had included an extra amount to cover the expenses of the car repairs.

"Jae, I know exactly what we should do with the rest of the money!"

Their day trip, now extended to a four-day holiday, filled their hearts with a bubbling sense of exuberance. As they cruised down the open highway, the wind tousled their hair, amplifying the feeling of liberation that neither of them had experienced in a while. The vibrant scenery whizzed past, painting a picturesque backdrop of rolling hills and lush greenery.

Pia couldn't help but visualize herself as the proud owner of Kramer's, the restaurant she had always admired. In her mind's eye, she saw it transformed into a charming and polished establishment brimming with life and love.

Anticipation filled the air, mingling with the scent of fresh air and adventure. With a deep breath, Pia eagerly prepared to share her dream, her voice trembling with excitement.

Jae, not waiting to hear, replied, "Yep. Me too! We're finally going to Wisconsin."

Pia smiled.

About The Author

Deena Kaye lives with a lot of cats, a few dogs, many plants and some very old books.

Deena also has a varied background in human services and emotional well-being training. The characters portrayed in her stories reflect real life, genuine feelings, and authentic life choices that fill the reader with sensory pleasures, laughter, and tears.

Living life, accepting what I know, changing what I can, embracing who I am, perseverates through my writings.

Always be the best you can be and love yourself, regardless.

Questions or comment are welcome at BlackWillowPub@gmail.com   A posted review from you would be greatly appreciated.